Credentials

The Complete Series

A BWWM BILLIONAIRE ROMANCE

Jaelynn McCranie

Publisher's Note: This is a work of fiction. Names,
characters, places and incidents are a product of
the author's imagination. Locales and public
names are sometimes used for atmospheric
purposes. Any resemblance to actual people, living
or dead, or to businesses, companies, events,
institutions, or locales is completely coincidental.

Credentials/ Jaelynn McCranie -- 1st ed.
Xplicit Press, an imprint of TLM Media LLC

ISBN-13: 978-1-62327-649-2
ISBN-10: 1-62327-649-7
eISBN: 978-1-62327-650-8

Printed in the United States of America

CONTENTS

1

L eah looks around her apartment, not feeling like she is in New York at all. She may as well be on Mars, or Jupiter, feeling totally cut off from life, and everything that she thought she knew to be true about herself. Her world has fallen apart, even though at 24, she should have her whole life in front of her. She feels that the best is behind her, however.

Her grandmother has just died, and a few months earlier, she lost her grandfather. She is every kind of cliché, absent father, crackhead mother, more brothers and sisters than she can count on one hand. She has managed to get away from the destruction, however, and work herself into her own apartment, with some sort of stability.

With her grandparents now dead, though, she realizes that the only stability she had was their love and the fact that she could go to their house on weekends for some soul food and a lot of love. She wonders what hope there is for her brothers now, all older than her, all already riding with gangs, proving every African American stereotype correct.

She has a few dreams, dreams that she had to put on the backburner while she worked herself out of the projects. Now, though, she feels like she has nothing to lose, nothing left for her in New York. Los Angeles appeals to her, not because she aspires to be an actress. She wants instead to be the force behind the styles and red carpet looks of celebrities, and she finally feels that she can make the move.

Moving your life across the country is no small feat, however, and Leah has a few loose ends to tie up. She has to report to her boss that she won't be coming back; she has to pack up her apartment, although this isn't too much work, and she has to let her friends know what she has decided. She decides that the best thing to do will be to lie, saying that she already has a job lined up for her in LA, just so that they will not give her too much grief about this huge decision.

Once she has made her decision, and solidified it in her head, however, she is surprised by how quickly she wraps up her life. There really isn't much to pack up, and she sees this as a sign that she is making the right choice. The ease with which she is able to remove herself from New York lets her know that her grandparents were probably the only thing that made her feel like she was rooted in this city. She books a bus ticket and gets to the station a full three hours before she is supposed to, at the risk of her changing her mind.

Leah arrives in Los Angeles just as the sun comes up over the ocean. It is beautiful, and she loses herself for a moment in this beauty. Then the reality of her situation hits her upside the head, and she needs coffee. She finds a coffee shop near the station and buys the paper. The LA Times is bulkier than its New York counterpart is, and she sees this as a gold mine of opportunity. So what if most of it is celebrity fluff, who cares? This is, after all, the world that she wants to lose herself in.

She needs to sleep but knows that there is no time to waste. Coming from the city that never sleeps, she wills herself awake, assuring herself that she will rest once she has at least managed to line up a few interviews. The money in her bank account will not last her very long, a month at most, and so she needs to get a job in a hurry. She has not even thought about where she is going to live in LA.

Leah looks at her mobile phone for the longest time, wishing it were eight o'clock already so that she could start making calls. LA stirs at 9 AM at the earliest, however, and she is on her fifth cup of coffee before somebody picks up the phone on the other end. She starts to work down her list of potential jobs. She has them divided into what she can do, and what she wants to do. The last list is just to keep her motivated, but you never know.

"Do you have an online portfolio? Who

have you dressed? What music videos have you styled?" The questions seem to come in quick succession from the confident voice of Ray Von Helsing, who placed an ad for a junior stylist in the Times.

"Nobody, but..." Leah starts to respond.

"Then I'm afraid I cannot help you. Get some work under your belt and call me again in six months." Ray puts the phone down, and Leah isn't sure if she just sounds irritated, or if she has just woken up. Her voice is raspy, like toast, so that either is possible.

Leah makes a few other calls, lining up a few interviews for the jobs she can do, but coming back to Ray Von Helsing's ad repeatedly. She decides to call her again, not knowing why, but knowing that she hopes for a different outcome.

"Ray Von Helsing?"

"Hello, this is Leah!"

"Leah?" Ray doesn't even recognize her voice. She must be inundated with calls, so early in the morning, and so Leah sees an opportunity. She decides to take a slightly different approach.

"Yes, Leah...I'd like to set up an

appointment!" One thing she knows about established stylists like Ray is that they cannot afford to alienate new talent. And they can never be sure of who everybody in the industry is, every day having its share of *It Girls* and *It Guys* coming out of the woodwork. Leah also knows that you don't make an appointment with Ray Von Helsing unless you know who you are.

"Let me see...I can see you at 12; we can make it a lunch thing. Leah, you say?"

"Yes, Leah... See you at 12!"

Her stomach hurts suddenly. The New Yorker in her is proud of herself for getting the appointment, being the new kid on the block. However, LA is a very different kettle of fish. She pays her bill and picks up her suitcase. After getting directions to the nearest internet café, she exits the coffee shop and feels the rush of the LA morning on her face. Anxiety quickly turns to excitement.

It is amazing how much information is available on the internet. By 11 AM, she knows everything about Ray Von Helsing, from what her favorite color is, to what she had for dinner last night.

She also knows what she likes to have for lunch, and just where to get it. After checking into the cheapest motel she can find, and dressing as well as her limited wardrobe will allow, she makes her way to Ray Von Helsing's boutique, armed with a chilled bottle of split lemon mineral water and a chicken salad.

The buzzer is intimidating so Leah takes a moment to catch her breath. Then she rings it, three long rings, to give the illusion of confidence. After a moment, the door buzzes open, so that Leah is suddenly off busy Rodeo Drive, and inside the luxury boutique, soaked with designer labels starting at the door.

She looks around for the person who opened up the door for her but sees nobody. She tries not to be star struck and gathers herself. Looking around the boutique, she isn't sure if she can even touch the garments hanging from the mannequins. The shop is set up like a store, but there are no price tags on any of the items. They are just to give clients an idea of what is out there. They are a window into what is fresh off the ramps of the world's

Fashion Weeks.

"Leah...hello!" Ray is beautiful. If she has had any work done, then it was done very well. She doesn't look a day over 30, although Leah knows from her biography online that she is closer to 45. *"You're alone?"*

She asks this question as though she expects Leah to have an entourage, in true Hollywood style. Leah almost expects *'her people'* to suddenly appear and touch up her makeup, or her hair. Nobody makes an appearance, however, and she has to suddenly be in the game, and give it the one shot she knows she has.

"Yes, I'm alone...I brought you lunch!"

"Excuse me?"

"Lunch... So that you can eat while we talk!" Leah is trying very hard for her confidence not to come across as arrogance.

"Okay...what can I help you with? Although, by the look of things, I cannot imagine that you need much help with styling!" Leah doesn't know if she is being serious, or if she is just humoring her. She takes a look at herself, a knee-length red dress, black heels and a silver clutch in her hand.

Leah looks presentable but hardly stylish, she thinks.

"I really want to work for you..." Leah cannot think of anything else to say, so she just comes out with it.

"Ah...and you think that a chicken salad will get you a job with me?" Ray is still eating the salad, however, so that is a good sign.

"Well, at least, I will not leave a bitter taste in your mouth!" Leah looks at her in her eyes, with everything inside her telling her to look away, her head telling her to hold Ray's gaze.

After the longest time, and Ray finishing up her salad, she lets out a chuckle. *"I take it you have no experience?"*

"No, but I learn very quickly, and as you can see, I have a certain style..."

"For New York, yes, but this is LA honey, and out here, we wear our dresses a little shorter than that!" Ray adjusts her own skirt, which sits about three inches above her knee. She looks like she is ready for a night out at a gala dinner, and not a day at the office. Given her office, however, it is not entirely unacceptable.

"I arrived from New York this

morning...left them for just that reason... their skirts are way too long!" They both laugh now, and the air finally makes its way to Leah's lungs.

"I like you... you're quick... I like that... I might have something for you after all!"

Ray decides to appoint Leah as her junior personal assistant. She spends the afternoon showing her how she runs her business and testing her on the phone. Leah really is a quick study, and in one afternoon, she has learned as much as would have taken a lesser mortal a couple of months. She leaves Ray at around 7 PM and takes a cab back to the motel. After all, she can afford it now that she has a job.

She could not have scripted it better herself. Her first day in Los Angeles, and already she has a job. She just needs to find an apartment now, something closer to work, and invest in a couple of shorter skirts. In the meantime, she will wear jeans and trousers, so as not to offend her new boss.

Ray calls Leah the next day and asks her to meet her at her house. After giving her the address, she hangs up without saying goodbye. Leah wonders what this means since she had already planned the best way, once again thanks to the internet, to get to work by bus. Now she has to spend more money on a cab all the way to Beverly Hills. Her stomach knots, but she knows that this is the new game she is going to have to play. This is a game that she is going to have to play well if she is to have any hope of making it in this town.

She wears a crisp white shirt and distressed denim jeans. A silver belt and silver heels add bling to the outfit, and she looks at as much of herself that she can see in the tiny bathroom mirror in the motel. Thankfully, there is a larger mirror in the lobby of the motel, and she takes a good look at herself. She looks casual and professional, as per Ray's instructions. Leah thinks she nailed the look.

"Are you sure?" the cabby asks her when she hands him the piece of paper with the address on it.

"Yes, I'm sure!" she says confidently, knowing of course that the transition from where she is to where she wants to go is an incredible one.

When the cab finally pulls up to the Von Helsing's house, Leah realizes the cabby's response to her little note. It is the most beautiful home in the cul-de-sac, and she takes a moment to take it all in before she presses the buzzer at the gate. When she finally does, a voice in a clear Spanish accent asks her for her credentials. Then there is a short conversation that she can't hear, and seconds later the large wrought iron gates vibrate and then open with a soft hum.

She walks up the long driveway, and by the time she reaches the front door, she has counted 20 grounds staff. Evidently, Ray could not have made all this money by styling celebrities. She must have married very rich, very, very wealthy. Leah stands in front of the intimidating front door and wonders whether she should use the knocker, or ring the doorbell.

The door swings open, and suddenly she has no time to be intimidated. A young Spanish maid holds the door open for her, and Leah steps inside the massive entrance hall. It is three times the size of her motel room, and she just takes it all in. There might never be time again for her to be in this space again, so she takes her time to absorb everything that she sees around her.

Ray meets her just as she exits the entrance hall, and she embraces her like an old friend, which takes Leah by surprise. She looks at the color of her hand, and cannot help but think that she should be a member of staff in uniform, and not standing here, air kissing this billionaire's wife. Ray walks her to the living room.

Karl Von Helsing is standing by the large French windows, with a drink in his hand that Leah thinks it is too early for him to be having. He looks twice age, with hair that seems to be almost too dark. After he greets her, Leah deduces that he is German, and the picture suddenly makes sense. She cannot help but think that he is nothing she would ever have considered for herself personally.

But he is not her husband, and seeing him standing next to Ray, they make the perfect couple actually. He is obviously filthy rich, and she is obviously just keeping herself busy with her little styling hobby. They must look very exquisite on the covers of the society pages. Leah makes a mental note to look for a few pictures of the couple on the internet.

"This is your first project...My husband needs to be at an awards thing in New York tonight, and he doesn't particularly trust my Los Angeles take on fashion...So I thought you might have some New Yorker insights for him. Just make him look good. I'll see you at the boutique in an hour!" Ray speaks in one long sentence, almost as though she is afraid that her words might get away from her.

"But..." Leah wants to protest. It's all just too much too soon. However, if she is to prove herself to Ray quickly, this is the perfect opportunity. She watches as Ray plants a long kiss on Karl's mouth so that she has to look away. Ray gives Leah a few instructions as to the do's and don'ts, and then leaves her alone with her husband.

Leah breathes deep, and then she decides to make her mark. She has no experience with styling anybody, but she has practiced enough times in her head to know that you start with what the person feels comfortable in. She only has an hour, and pictures of Karl Von Helsing will probably be in every New York paper, come tomorrow. She needs to make this work.

Karl leads her to his dressing room, the biggest she has ever seen, and just points out the suits. Many of them still have the tags on them, so Leah knows that this is where she must start. He needs to be seen in something that he has not worn yet.

Confidently, he begins to undress, so that Leah wants to protest. Before she can, though, he is standing in front of her in nothing but his underwear, very expensive looking Klein's, and she turns to the suits and wishes that she could just disappear behind them.

"I'm all yours," Karl says smugly, knowing that what he has just said is drenched in innuendoes. Leah pretends not to see this, pulling items from their hangers, and trying not to look at Karl's rather impressive crotch.

Soon enough, he has clothes on, though, and she is relieved. A navy Hermes suit, with a dusty blue shirt, and a dark blue tie. He looks like he just stepped off the cover of a top fashion magazine, or Times. She searches for conversation, but comes up with nothing, so she just gets on with putting together three more looks for Karl.

"So, you are a New Yorker?" Karl asks her, the German still thick in his accent. He is already in his underwear again, ready for the next experiment. People in Los Angeles really had a way of existing in perfect bubbles where they were perfect, and everyone else around them was just an accessory. Leah feels like an accessory.

"Yes..." Leah manages, looking through the large stained windows of the dressing room, trying hard again not to look at Karl's penis. It is just such an impressive penis that she cannot help herself stealing a few gazes. She catches herself measuring it, easily twelve inches, maybe more she thinks. She shakes the image from her head, and moves her mind to the matter at hand, wondering if she will make it a whole hour with this man, and not wanting to touch him. She suddenly really wants to touch him...

2

"*Well done, **miss thang**!*" Ray tries to mimic the way African Americans speak but fails dismally. She holds up the front page to the New York Times, a picture of Karl Von Helsing on it. He made the front page. What does this man do, she wonders?

"*Thank you...*" Leah says after she checks that he wore the outfit exactly as they decided. Not that Karl was on the front page of the New York Times because of her choice of clothing mind you, but that is the only thing a real stylist looks at.

"*There might be hope for you yet. We have a gala dinner tonight...and I want you to style both of us."*

"Does that mean I'm a stylist now?" Leah cannot help but ask the question, even though it is only her third day here.

"Honey, you won't be a stylist for a while yet. Consider this the internship to your internship. You are still very much just a junior personal assistant!" The words coming out of her mouth cut Leah, even though she winks at her, letting her know that she might just take a short cut to the top if she does a good job with Ray and Karl Von Helsing tonight.

The new Versace low back makes quick work of Ray's styling. Leah moves effortlessly through the boutique, as if she knows it inside out already, and assembles the accessories that will go with the dress she has chosen for Ray. Ray seems pleased, albeit a little surprised by some of Leah's choices. Although she has to admit to herself that, they actually work.

She has to go to Karl at the house to style him, even though she already knows from memory just what he should be wearing. Ray insists, however that she go and make sure that everything looks the way they see it in their heads. Karl is available, and at home for a couple of hours, so after Leah packs up the dress, she is in a cab and on her way to the Von Helsing mansion.

Leah arrives to find Karl having another early drink. She wonders if his eyes are just naturally glassy or if perhaps it is this habit that gives him that dreamy look. After greeting him, she goes straight up to his dressing room and removes the clothing that she has her mind set on. They all still have their tags on them, so that she knows that at least there will be no internet references for them. She puts the dress next to this ensemble and stands back to admire her handy work. She really does have a knack for this.

"*Nice,*" Karl says, already stripped down to his underwear by the time Leah turns around.

"*You like it? Good! There will be no need for you to fit anything on, I just came by to make sure that...*" She loses the words as Karl comes in close enough for her to feel his breath on her face. She can smell the gin.

"Do you like it?" He asks her the question while throwing his eyes down to when his penis is starting to strain against the fabric of his underwear.

Leah isn't sure if she is seeing things, and if perhaps she is really seeing what she is seeing. There is a moment where Leah even thinks that she is dreaming and that her new boss's husband could not possibly be hitting on her. Any doubt that she has goes right out the window, however, as soon as Karl takes her hand and holds it against his almost hard cock. The dick that seemed to be struggling to rise is suddenly fully erect almost as soon as Leah's hand lands on it.

Karl is impressed. He did not think that this is the effect that Leah's fingers would have on his meat. Leah is surprised and shocked, but also intrigued at the effect that she has on this man she would not have looked at twice anywhere but here. The moment lingers, and then Leah quickly pulls her hand off Karl. She really has nothing to say to him.

She starts to gather the clothing, needing to get them to the cleaners just so that they don't have that *'new-*

straight-off-the-rack' look. She makes it to the bedroom door, but then Karl is in front of her, saying with his eyes what is not necessary for him to say with his mouth. Leah just shakes her head, telling Karl to move out of her way with her eyes.

He questions her request with his own eyes, and she has no response but to giggle. She remembers suddenly reading somewhere that Germans, in particular, had a fascination for darker skins, but this is wrong on so many levels. Perhaps another place, another time, she might have entertained this possibility. This situation is certainly not that place or time.

Her eyes fall to where Karl now has his cock in his hands. He is the kind of arrogant that you would find attractive if you were 16. Still, she stirs in places that she cannot help, and her eyes rest on the massive meat between his long, thick fingers. Karl moves in close to her, and for a brief moment, she lets him come close enough to kiss her. Just then, however, she turns her face and rushes passed the small gap in the doorway.

She has to catch her breath outside

before she gets into the car that brought her here. She lets her eyes find the driver's crotch, suddenly needing to be touched. Leah manages, however, to bring herself forward and make it to the dry cleaners. Then she manages to distract herself with a quick lunch at a Chinese restaurant near the cleaners, thinking that she may as well wait for the clothing. She will not take them back to the mansion. However, the thought of Karl waiting for her locked and loaded too much for her.

Leah thinks better of telling Ray about her husband's advances. She decides that this is Hollywood, and she is going to have to put her big girl panties on. The underwear she has on now though is practically soaked, flooded with the juices of the arousal she hadn't fully allowed herself to process. She must just make it through this afternoon.

Back in her motel room, Leah heads straight for the shower and puts her fingers on herself. She tries to imagine anyone else but Karl touching her, but images of his cock keep coming into her head so that she is practically pulling on her clit. She imagines that he is an aggressive lover if his ego and arrogance are anything to go by. She lets images of him play out in her head while her fingers make quick work of her aching pussy.

Ray and Karl look spectacular at the event that evening, she catches it on the TV. She undresses Karl with her mind, against her own better judgment. She brings herself to climax twice more during the night, each time because Karl has appeared on the TV in a highlights segment from the event's red carpet. She makes the decision never to be alone with him again, knowing now that she will not be able to resist him if he made a pass at her one more time.

However, Karl seems persistent and requests another meeting with Leah. He needs three looks for a European film festival, which has Leah wondering again just what he does. She assumes that he has various interests, or that, like most businessmen with their fingers in many pies, that Karl Von Helsing just has to make appearances at the various ventures that have his money as their backbone.

"Are you sure?" She asks Ray,

hoping that her boss will say no and just style her husband herself.

"Yes, of course, go for it! Karl always makes use of my stylists, and since you're the closest thing to a stylist that I have on my books at the moment, it only makes sense. Go..." Ray is more confident than she should be, Leah thinks.

"About that..." she starts, needing to know if she has not yet proven herself as a stylist yet. It has hardly been two weeks, however, but Leah is ambitious.

"Look, honey...Do right by my husband, and then we can talk about that stylist position. You're doing a good job so far, but there are some rules to the game that you still need to learn; and how better to learn them than with someone whose style has a direct impact on my image?" Leah tries not to read between the lines, because if she does, then Ray is telling her to sleep with her husband. She could not possibly be saying that, however.

She arrives at the mansion, dressed in jeans and a shirt, trying in vain to downplay her sexuality. She arrives just after nine AM, and after exchanging pleasantries with Karl, who is having a plate of actual fruit for breakfast, she rushes up the stairs to the dressing room to look through Karl's clothing.

Leah takes some the clothing off the rack and starts to separate them into two piles, one for *'hell no's'* and one for *'maybes'*. She finds herself looking at the crotches in every pair of pants and running her fingers across this area of the fabric. She remembers how his cock felt in her hands, and again she is suddenly very warm between her legs.

She tries to come back into the moment and to focus on what she is here to do. There is no time for this, however because Karl is standing in the room, watching her running her fingers over the groin areas of his trousers. He knows that he has her in his grip now and that it won't be long before he gets a taste of the berry that lies between her thighs.

"You like?" he asks, watching her fingers now, and not her eyes.

"Uhm...yes, the fabric is beautiful!" She tries to distract him from what she knows he is actually asking her.

"You know what I mean. Come now, Leah, you're a clever girl. I don't think,

or at least, I hope that you are not naïve." Karl exudes confidence. Leah might not be physically attracted to him, but she is definitely drawn to him because of this trait. He comes over to her and puts his hand over her hand, and presses her fingers down in the crotch of the pants that she is holding up. She is almost disappointed that there is nothing there.

He guides her hand to his actual penis again, and she cannot say that she is disappointed. Everything in her is telling her to get away from this man who is determined to get into her panties, but she is already entertaining the possibility of sleeping with him. She thinks of Ray and tries to lift her hand off the hard meat. Karl presses her hand down harder so that she wraps her fingers around the thick dick.

"There's a good girl!" Karl says, seeming to almost lose his breath.

She doesn't make the conscious decision to do this, but then she drops the pants in her free hand, and she goes down on her knees. She unwraps the package that is practically aching for her to touch it, and then she places the fingers of both her hands on the massive dick in front of her. She looks at the door, still wide open, almost expecting a maid to come through the door at any moment.

Karl plants his feet firmly in the soft carpet and reaches behind him so that he touches the side of the door and manages to slide it closed. The lights in the room suddenly come on, sensors letting them know that there are people in the room, and so the space is flooded with light. She closes her eyes and tries to think of anything but what is actually happening. She opens her mouth and places the massive head on his dick between her lips and starts to work her way down the shaft.

It is hot in her mouth, hotter than she expected it to be. For a moment, she cannot believe that she is actually doing this, but then Karl hits the back of her throat so that she needs to focus on the matter of this oral transaction. Briefly, she wonders what the situation will be between them after he cums, but there is no turning back now. She sends her tongue around the head and is surprised when pre-cum trickles onto the tip of it. He really wants her.

She takes a deep breath and slides the dick all the way into her mouth again, as far as it will go. It settles more comfortably in the back of her mouth, and he thrusts slightly, lodging it firmly so that no air can pass through the back of her mouth anymore. She lets it settle there for a moment, and then slowly moves her lips back up to his head.

Anxiety comes over her in waves, and then it gives way to excitement. She cannot believe that she has this German meat in her mouth, and her curiosity gets the better of her. Leah has had lovers in the past, but they have all been African-American. She had heard stories about the endowments of white men, but all those myths are shot to hell now, with a solid 12-inch boner between her teeth.

Leah actually has to open her eyes, to make sure that the man on whose dick she is sucking is actually white. He is, and she notices that the throbbing cock has a blue vein running up the top of it. It is red, bordering on purple, and it is rock hard. Age and early morning drinking have clearly not had an effect on this man's libido.

Karl settles into this rather quickly. His moans let her know as much. Leah too is becoming more and more comfortable with this meat in her mouth so that she is also moaning now. Karl watches her go to work on his cock, and he is thrilled that she is finally in it. He holds her hair back so that he can watch her lips wrap around his cock and slide up and down his shaft.

Then he takes her by her shoulders. He lifts her gently, but insistently, so that she has to find her footing and comes to standing. She is again taken aback by how tall he is, her head barely making it to the hairy man's chest. She looks at the man's chest, not sure if she should take his thick nipples in her mouth. She goes for it, realizing that there is really no turning back now. If she is going to lose her job, she may as well go out in a balling flame.

The curls that she finds there are soft, and they smell of vanilla and tobacco. She has never seen Karl smoke, but he obviously does, if this scent is anything to go by. She hates cigarettes, but smelling this on Karl is strangely erotic, so that she is really wet now. She aches for Karl to put his hands on her softness, and she regrets suddenly that she decided to wear jeans.

Karl makes light work of her pants, however, and soon enough she is just standing in front of him in nothing but panties and her bra. She cannot help herself but check that he has not just thrown her clothing on the floor, already thinking about the aftermath of this liaison, and knowing that she needs to be as put together as when she reported for work this morning. Karl has managed to place her clothing neatly on the center table in the elegant dressing room.

Now Karl is on his knees, his fingers holding her panties and pulling them away from her skin. He pulls them down slowly so that she almost wants to tell him to hurry up. She doesn't however, knowing somehow that he needs to be in full control of this interaction if she is to walk away from it with some of her conscience intact. Soon enough, though, she is stepping out of her panties as they finally reach her ankles.

Karl practically swallows her cunt, sending his tongue so deep inside her that she gasps. He has a powerful tongue, long, thick and wet. It is also very hot so that she feels this warmth up the length of her spine. She can honestly say that she has never been gone down on this way before, and she feels like she could explode at any moment. She doesn't however, and soon enough she is grinding her feminine bits into the depths of Karl's mouth.

He seems to nibble on her clit forever, but each bite is unique so that she feels like he has just started. She holds onto the top of his head, her fingers gripping his perfectly conditioned hair as he goes to town on her pussy. For a moment, she allows herself to forget where she is, and who she is with. She cannot allow guilt to take over her now because she really needs this. She really wants this.

Then Karl is back on his feet, and feeding her the taste of herself with his mouth. His tongue really is thick, and it fills her mouth so that she almost feels like she cannot breathe. Just before she feels like she might lose consciousness, he removes his tongue from her mouth and plants the softest kisses on her lips. She doesn't expect him to be such a great kisser since he hardly has lips, but then she realizes that she is just comparing him with her other lovers, and she decides not to knock it until she has tried it completely.

Her eyes are still closed, and Karl is watching her closely now. He stares at her for a long time until she opens her eyes when it seems like he has stopped touching her. As soon as her eyes open, she meets his gaze, and her eyes remain open. He has a piercing stare and the most beautiful eyes. She cannot pull away from them. Then she feels her pussy filling suddenly so that she is almost embarrassed by how easily this intrusion fills her. She really is very wet.

Karl sends his finger all the way up her, and then moves it around as though he is searching for something. She hopes that he never finds what he is looking for, feeling butterflies all over her skin so that she practically quivers. There is a moment where Karl pauses so that it is Leah who is grinding against this finger inside her. Then suddenly it is as if Karl finds the treasure that he was searching for, and Leah loses her footing and collapses in Karl's arms. He has found her g-spot!

She runs her fingers up and down his shaft now, letting Karl know that she wants him inside her. He throws his eyes around the room, realizing that his own trousers are not in the room, and, therefore, neither is his wallet. He will just have to be careful not to cum inside her in the absence of a condom. He really wishes that he had planned this better.

There is a moment where she thinks he might change his mind as he pulls his finger from inside her and just looks at her. She wishes suddenly that she could hide her face. He asks her with his eyes if she is sure. She isn't sure what her response is, but soon enough Karl is lifting her off the ground. He places her on the table and then pulls her towards his waiting dick. He also really wants to be inside her now.

The stretch is almost uncomfortable due to the thickness of Karl's meat.

Leah wants him all inside her, however, and she makes her own adjustments to allow this. He is excited now; he can't help it, or hide it. He thrusts quickly into her until after a few hard thrusts he is all the way inside her. She is stretched far back in her vagina so that she feels him almost all the way into her chest. It is a beautiful feeling.

Karl really goes for it now, so that he grunts uncontrollably. If anybody were to come into the bedroom now, they would know immediately what is happening. Leah has lost count of how many orgasms she has in quick succession. Still she is not satisfied. She wants him to eat the shit out of her so that she can leave this room without the need that has consumed her since the first time she caught the outline of his cock in his Klein's.

He does, and soon enough he is at the point of no return. She knows that if they were anywhere else, this might have lasted longer. It doesn't need to, however, the feeling in her cunt bordering on pain now as he milks every last drop of the juice inside it out. Then suddenly he is out of her, and pulling her off the table so that she can take his meat in her mouth once more. The mess that would result otherwise would be difficult to explain.

She tastes herself on his cock, and this too turns her on incredibly. She has her own fingers on her cunt now, and with the focus of a rocket scientist, brings herself to one last climax. Then all the attention is on the cock between her lips, and she determines to milk him as much as he milked her. With both her hands moving up and down his shaft the keeps his head in her mouth. The meat starts to throb so that she knows he is close.

Finally, he starts to roar and spills a massive amount of cum into her mouth, and down her throat. She has to swallow quickly, the sheer volume of the white fluid coming from this man incredible. She swallows three more times, and then she is licking the head clean. She is almost proud of herself for the great job that she just did. He looks like he is very proud of himself.

She dresses quickly, unable to look at Karl. He is composed and calm, and after covering himself up, he pulls the suggested outfits that he likes from the ones she has chosen. Nothing is said about what just happened, and once she is happy with the three looks, she excuses herself and makes for the front door. The day seems different to her somehow now so that it feels like even the trees know what she has just done.

Leah gets back to the boutique and loses herself in admin tasks. Ray is out for the afternoon, thank god, and when she doesn't return by four, she just locks up and heads back to her motel. She heads straight for the bathroom, and has a long shower, trying hard not to think about Karl, but thinking of nothing else. How could this happen, and so quickly? She thinks that she has ruined any chances of making it in Hollywood now, allowing herself to give into lust with another woman's husband.

Then she realizes that this is Hollywood, and things like this happen all the time. Ray probably knows about her husband's tastes but chooses to keep quiet. She tries to find many justifications for what she has just done, but none of them sits well with her. She decides not to think about it too much, and after a quick dinner of coffee and a bagel, she is back in her motel room, lying on the bed, naked, thinking of Karl Von Helsing's massive penis inside her, and wondering, just wondering if it will happen again.

The next time she sees Karl he greets her with the detachment that he always seems to have. Nothing about the way they interact gives any indication of the fucking that took place in his dressing room just a few days earlier. Perhaps it is because Ray is in the room, perhaps not. Leah is confused by this, and she starts to think that maybe she was just a once-off and she probably just helped the middle-aged *sonofabitch* empty his massive sack.

She watches him interact with his wife, and isn't sure if what she is seeing is love or familiarity. Whatever it is, it starts to get under her skin, so that she wishes that she was nothing more than a tea girl at Ray Von Helsing's boutique and that she never set eyes on her husband in their home. No wishing in the world will make this go away, though, and Leah cannot help the thoughts that creep up on her unexpectedly. She wants Karl to fuck her again. She needs him to fuck her. She starts to think how she can make this happen, or if in fact, he will give in to her advances if she is the aggressor.

3

month goes by with Leah and Karl not being left alone. She starts to accept that it was a one-time thing, and she focuses on her work now. She has also managed to get a studio apartment near her work, which takes her mind of the German dick that rocked her world. She has not even seen him in about two more weeks, and she assumes that he is either avoiding her or off making his billions.

Then unexpectedly she gets a message on her voicemail. Ray needs her to go straight to her house to help Karl get ready for the annual general meeting of one of his many companies. She wants to decline, thinking of many reasons why she cannot go. She can think of one reason why she should go, however, and this trumps all the other lies she is telling herself. Her mind is suddenly fresh with the memory of their little dressing room tryst.

"You've been scarce!" Karl says, trying to get a feel for where her head is.

"I've been busy!" Leah cannot think of anything more.

"My wife really does work all her girls really hard!" Leah hears the innuendos in what he is saying but quickly dismisses them, at the risk of feeling like a prostitute.

"That she does!" She manages a suitable response, she thinks.

"I've thought of you often!" He starts down the path that she hoped he would not go down.

"You shouldn't, it was a mistake!" An attack of conscience forces the words out.

"A mistake I'd like to make again..." Karl lets his words hang around her head and watches as they warm the space between her thighs.

She wants to object, but Karl is already on her. He overwhelms her with his size and the fact that he is already naked. She wishes suddenly that he did not have so many unused items of clothing in his closet so that they could have gone shopping, and been out in public. She thinks that this would somehow have made it easier for her to resist him.

Leah is wearing a light summer dress, and she immediately regrets this. His hands are underneath it quickly, and he is feeling for the moisture he found the last time he had his hands between her thighs. *"I see you want me to make this mistake again..."* He confirms what he knows to be true. She cannot hide the fact that she wants him. *"Don't worry, I'm prepared this time,"* He says this as he reaches for his pants on the table and pulls out a pack of condoms from his back pocket. Well, thought out infidelity was somehow acceptable in Los Angeles.

She watches as he rolls the condom over his shaft, no foreplay this time, probably due to the time constraints. Leah tries to look away from him as he lifts her dress and pulls her panties to the side to allow him to access her cunt. This is not how she had played it out in her head over the many times that she allowed herself to fantasize about the *next time,* but she reminds herself that there is just no time for anything else. He feeds her his finger and moves it around inside her while he turns her face to his.

He kisses her full on the mouth. His kisses are different this time, fuelled it seems with passion and longing. He moves his tongue around inside her mouth and then takes her tongue in his mouth. Then he feeds her another finger, increasing the stretch, making sure that she is warm and ready. She moistens considerably so that Karl can comfortably add a third finger. He parts his fingers inside her slightly, just to make sure that she will receive him easier this time.

His lips don't leave hers as he slowly removes his fingers. He lifts her onto her tiptoes and then parts her legs slightly. Then he lowers her slowly onto his cock, one finger keeping her panties to the side until he has gained entry. After a third of his cock is inside her, he presses down gently on her shoulders with both hands until he is all the way up inside her. She cannot breathe.

Slowly at first, he starts to thrust, drawing more and more of her own juices from her vaginal walls. As it becomes easier to move inside her, he intensifies his thrusting. Already Leah feels like she is going to cum, and she braces herself on his arms. He keeps thrusting at a consistent pace, determined to satisfy her before he lets himself go.

Then his dick is moving in wide circles inside her, as though he were stirring a teacup. Then it is moving up and down as though he were settling a thick pin in the soft cushion that is the back of her cunt. She cannot believe how good this man that is not hers feels inside her, and she hides her face in his chest. Kissing him allows her to think that there is more happening here than just illicit sex, and so she tries to avoid it.

Karl is determined to enjoy every bit of her, however, and again he is holding her face so that she cannot escape his lips. His thrusts don't skip a beat, and soon enough she is cumming again, afraid that she might get some of her juices on the carpet. Karl keeps at it, thrusting long, hard and deep now so that she knows that he is going to cum soon too. Thanks to the condom, he can reach is climax inside her. She wants this.

He lifts her dress completely above her waist now and grabs hold of her butt. He is really going for it now, and the roaring noises coming from his mouth let her know that it won't be long now. She cums again, however before he finally lets himself blow. He keeps his dick inside her until it starts to go soft, and then slowly extracts it. The condom looks set to burst for all the cum inside it. He really shoots an impressive load.

After making minor adjustments to herself, she looks as fresh as she did when she walked into the room. Karl is fitting on the clothing that she has laid out for him. Not a word is spoken about what just happened, but Leah puts this off as his conscience. She just hopes that his conscience does not bother him enough for him to tell his wife that he fucked the shit out the help, twice.

Leah realizes that she has a bit of a hold on Karl, even though he has not said as much. She allows her confusion to give way to confidence, and it shows in the way Leah starts to behave. She makes adjustments to her wardrobe, and slight modifications to her makeup even, so that she is slightly less timid, and more vixen. She is careful not to change too much, though, in case Karl actually likes the subtle vulnerability that she knows she still exudes.

Ray doesn't notice the changes, however, and this worries Leah. She craves the approval of this woman who has her life in the palm of her hands, and she needs to consistently make a good impression. Ray is so focused on her business, however that there really isn't time for her to pay attention to subtle changes in her PA's appearance. There is another thing on her mind too, mind you.

Karl and Ray have a very healthy sex life. They make love often, sometimes two or three times a night, when Karl is home. So one thing she is convinced of is that he is not cheating. How could he be? There is just so much energy in her husband, and he seems to spend it all on her.

However, over the last while, Karl has become slightly more aggressive as a lover. Where he used to make love to her, he now seems to have added a series of twists to their lovemaking. Where the sex was limited largely to the bedroom, suddenly he fucks her in the kitchen, and more recently, in their swimming pool. He caught her by complete surprise both times so that she is not sure if she enjoyed it, or if she was just indulging him.

The other day, he took her on the stairs. There were maids in the house, but they all seemed to be oblivious to what was going on. Not that he was completely naked mind you, or she, he just whipped out his penis and lifted her dress, filling her quickly on the landing and bring her to an incredible orgasm. She has no idea where this new twist comes from, but she assumes that he is just acting out his midlife crisis.

She reasons that it is better that he plays out these scenes in their home, and not on the front page of the many tabloids that are just waiting for the mighty Von Helsing to make a public faux pas. She remembers him even wetting the tip of his cock with spit when she didn't seem to get wet fast enough, but she assumes that this was for her pleasure as much as his. Still, this change bothers her slightly, so that she just has to talk to someone about it.

"*Are you okay?*" Leah asks when she notices that her boss is looking more distracted than usual.

"*Just a little overwhelmed, that's all!*" Ray isn't sure if she should be discussing her private life with her PA.

"*Is there anything I can do?*" Leah really is just relieved that Ray did not just say that she knows about her liaisons with her husband, and she's fired!

"*Well, can you keep a secret?*" Ray suddenly comes in close, as though she were going to reveal top-secret information to Leah.

"*Of course,*" Leah says, confidently, although she has never been entrusted with any sort of secret before.

Ray proceeds to whisper her husband's sexual appetites and

expectations to Leah, not giving her a chance to respond. She actually doesn't want a response of any sort from her, just to listen, and then to forget entirely everything that she has just heard. Leah listens intently. However, her imagination places her in each of the scenarios described by Ray so that she is once again wet and warm where it matters. She crosses her legs, leaning on her knees, hoping that the smell of her pheromones does not make it to Ray's nose.

As soon as Ray is done talking, Leah clears her throat, an indication that she was listening. Ray reminds her of the sensitivity of this information, and thanks her for being there for her to talk to. After asking her about her own non-existent love life, Ray suggests that they get back to work. She has no need to remind Leah not to mention this to Karl, assuming incorrectly that they discuss nothing beyond whether he should wear a tie or not to the next event.

Leah starts to realize that she is not taking Karl from Ray to the contrary in fact. She starts to see herself as an ally to this woman whose husband she is bedding. She gets Karl to relieve some of his stress and built up sexual tension with her, and then go back to his wife and make standard love to her in their bed in the missionary position. She decides there and then to avail herself for him whenever he calls her so that Ray can return her focus to her boutique, and to, hopefully, making her a stylist someday soon.

She decides to elevate her bedroom skills and to really wear Karl out the next time he is with her. She is curious to see how this will translate into Ray's own sex life. She buys books, and videos, to learn more than what she thinks she already knows about pleasing a man. Some things surprise her, some don't, but one thing is clear, that there are many ways to please Karl, and she plans to use them.

The next time Karl wants to fuck her, she decides, she will control the impulse to let him inside her. She will insist on a hotel so that she can have the luxury and convenience of a bed on which to play out some of the scenes that are filling her head already. She hopes that it will be soon, but according to a phone call she overheard between Ray and Karl, he is in Europe for two weeks. She uses the time to perfect some of the tricks she wants to apply to him upon his return.

A voicemail asks her to meet him at his house, something about him needing to put together a look for an awards function. She wonders how it is that he manages to make it through so many events and still make so much money and still be drinking by nine in the morning, but these are the least of her worries. She needs to put on a brave front, a strong resistance to this man who is fast becoming irresistible to her. She meets him at his house, but not before she has gone back to her apartment to change into jeans and a blouse. This should limit his access to her warm place.

"So, did you miss me?" Karl asks Leah, already removing his clothing. Leah just turns away and looks through what is left in his wardrobe that still has tags on. Karl comes up behind her, holds her close, and presses his man meat against her thigh.

"No Karl, not here. This is your home, your bedroom, the space you share with

your wife!" She tries to sound like she really means what she is saying. What she actually wants him to do is undress her and spread her wide on the table, or on the carpet.

"Are you okay?" he asks her, suddenly confused.

"I'm fine...we just cannot do this here, not anymore!" She places the items of clothing on the table and leaves the room before she loses her resolve. As she walks downstairs, she hopes that he will come running after her, or, at least, call her back. He doesn't, and soon enough she is back in the boutique, distracting herself with paperwork.

Shortly after five, she leaves the boutique, and within half an hour she is at home, staring at the Chinese takeout she got for dinner. She has almost fallen asleep when the text to meet Karl at the Hyatt comes through. He's done with his awards thing, and he really needs to see her. After a quick shower, she makes for the hotel.

She finds Karl in the room, already naked, lying on the bed. Leah wonders how different it will be to make love to him on a bed. She wonders if there will be more attention to detail, and to the other elements of lovemaking that are not just about penetration. She reasons that she only has a couple of hours before this man has to be back at home, making love to his wife, and her falling asleep in his arms.

She slips off her dress without saying a word to him. He just looks at her, lust hanging heavy in his eyes. There is also a hint of anxiety, which she correctly attributes to him having to be home in a couple of hours. He really does love his wife, and the last thing he wants is to hurt her just because he cannot keep his cock out of this black beauty. She walks over to the bed and gets into it, between his legs.

Karl bends his knees, wanting her to mount him quickly so that he can feel her warmth on his cock quickly. She bends down in front of his dick so that it practically fills her face. She goes down to his balls and runs her tongue over them slowly. He jerks, not expecting this. It's been a while since somebody licked his balls.

Leah takes one of them in her mouth and plays around with it. She runs her tongue over the soft flesh covering the orb. Then she takes the second one in her mouth and runs her tongue over the flesh covering both balls. Karl bends his knees completely now and then straightens his legs. He wraps them around Leah's head so that she sucks his nutsack deep into her throat. He groans loudly.

He watches her come up off his sack and trace up the back of his cock with the tip of her tongue. She holds the massive dick up with one hand, and then traces back down the shaft so that she is once again licking his balls. Then she is sucking them again, driving Karl insane, but before long, she is working up the meat with her tongue again.

Time is not on their side; she knows this. But she just needed to let him know that she is quite capable of paying close attention to the little things. He watches as his cock disappears into her mouth, and the feeling of pressure from every angle is amazing. Then she runs rings around the head of his cock with her tongue, right before she is swallowing it again. He could just lay there for hours if they had the time.

She manages to get to the condoms on the side table, and she unwraps one. She puts it on him, his cock hardening even more with the anticipation. Leah then straddles Karl and places his cock at the entrance to her vagina. Slowly, very slowly, she eases herself down on it, and the look on Karl's face says that he is privy to every inch of his meat disappearing inside Leah. She bends down to take his nipples in her mouth.

Leah starts to grind in small circles on the cock inside her, extracting loud moans from Karl. It has been a while since he has had someone ride him, and it brings back every good memory of sex that he has. Then she is grinding in larger circles, bringing his cock out of her somewhat, and then it is all inside her again. Karl places his hands on her hips, then on her butt, but he does not need to move her in any way on himself. She is doing a stellar job all on her own.

When Karl cums, it is a massive explosion, so that she wishes that she had placed a towel underneath him. Even the condom cannot hold the vast amounts of cum spewing out of his dick. Karl is speechless, a look of complete satisfaction on his face. Leah brings herself to a final climax, and then she slides off him. She cleans him up and then goes into the bathroom to sort herself out. When she comes out of the shower, Karl is not in the room, and he did not even leave her a note.

Leah decides to sleep in the bed, just to breathe him in. What is it about him that has her feeling this way? He is obviously just using her for sex, and she knows this. Why then, does she keep coming back for more? She resolves to build some sort of a social life for herself and work hard at getting this married man out of her system.

Karl goes home and plays out the scene that he just had with Leah on his wife. Ray is awkward on top of him at first, but soon enough, she is getting the hang of it. Unlike Leah however, he has to move her around on his dick, his wife lacking the rhythm and agility of the 24-year old. Nonetheless, she really enjoys it. He does too!

"He has never asked me to do that before...I kind of liked it!" Ray cannot wait to tell Leah of this new sexual

beast that she has in her bedroom. She goes on to inform her of every new trick that Karl seems to have added to his arsenal, tricks that Leah knows all too well. She manages to look surprised, though, so Ray has no reason to raise an eyebrow. Her efforts have backfired, however, and she wonders if Karl is just comparing her to his wife, or using her for practice.

"*Are you seeing anyone?*" Ray asks her one day, catching her by complete surprise.

"*Uhm, no...I'm just only now settling into life in LA, you know!*" Leah responds, hoping that she doesn't see the discomfort she is feeling at this invasion.

"*Well, it's about time you met someone...and I have just the guy in mind for you...unless you prefer girls?*" Ray squints at her attempt at a joke.

"*No...no...guys are good. Guys are very good. You don't have to go out of your way for me. I'll get in the game soon enough I'm sure.*" Leah really does not want to be discussing this with Ray, given what she knows she is doing with her husband.

"*Oh, I insist. Tell you what, I'll have a*

bit of a dinner party thing, and introduce the two of you casually. If you like him, then you like him. If you don't, then it won't be awkward. So, are you in?" Ray can have a way of saying something without asking, instead telling you what you are going to do.

"Okay...when?" Leah asks, seeing an opportunity to get even with Karl for leaving her in the hotel room without even saying goodbye. Who knows, she might even like this new man, and he might take her mind off the unattainable Karl Von Helsing.

"Next Tuesday? How does that suit you?"

"Next Tuesday is fine!" Leah needs this conversation to be about something else now; she cannot continue discussing this with Ray.

Tuesday comes quickly, and Leah wonders what she is going to wear. She cannot look like she put in too much of an effort, and yet she cannot be expected not to make any effort at all. By that afternoon, she had decided on a black cocktail dress that she bought to reward herself when she got her first paycheck. It is perfectly acceptable attire for a casual dinner party. She looks almost cheeky!

She arrives at the Von Helsing's house, shortly after seven, and takes a deep breath before ringing the doorbell. Karl opens up, and looks at the parts of her legs that are exposed where the dress stops suddenly. She lets his eyes linger, and then she comes up to him for the standard air kiss as soon as she catches Ray in her peripheral. Then she greets Ray and plants kisses on the left and right of her head.

Ray pulls her into the house and through to the back terrace, where the other guests are. She introduces Leah around and then taps a young man on his shoulder. When he turns around Leah is impressed at Ray's taste. He is the dark, broody sort of handsome that you wouldn't notice at first. He is obviously Latino, and he ticks every one of the boxes that Leah had growing up. This is a perfect distraction from Karl Von Helsing, she thinks. She hugs him while throwing her eyes around to see whether Karl has noticed her yet.

4

Karl has seen her, but he manages to hide his frustration at this couple very well. That is exactly what they look like, Leah and Manuel, who is an up and coming actor who just landed a huge role in a Hollywood epic of *Twilight* proportions. They act like a couple too, which surprises Leah. She had not expected that she would be so comfortable with him after the first meeting.

Karl keeps his eyes on Leah and imagines Manuel moving his hands on her. His mind strays to that place where he sees her doing with Manuel all the things that she has done to him.

He tries to shake this image from his head, but it is becoming harder and harder to do. With the dinner party in full swing now, Leah is giving all her attention to Manuel. He hates it but manages to hide it well.

Leah needs the bathroom, and Karl sees a gap. As soon as Leah disappears around a corner, he gets up and follows her. Karl checks to see that Ray doesn't notice, but she is occupied with her guests. Now is the perfect time to show Leah that he is the only man who knows how to make her feel good.

He waits for her outside the cloakroom, and as soon as she comes out, he pulls her into the library next to his study. They really just have a few minutes before Ray or Manuel come looking for them, but a few minutes is all Karl needs. He puts a finger on Leah's lips and locks the library door. He will make this quick, but he will also make this very good.

Karl places his hand on her thigh and slides it up to her cunt. She wants to object, but at the same time; she is experiencing all the butterflies that she has always felt whenever Karl has his hands on her. He pulls her panties down to her knees and goes down on his. After pulling her dress over his head, he digs deep into her pussy with his tongue, sending immediate shards of pleasure through her whole body.

She is wet quickly, and Karl makes quick work of wrapping his dick tightly in the condom he had already in his back pocket. He comes up to standing and places his mouth on hers while he finds her hotness with his cock. Karl enters her quickly and starts thrusting wildly, spurred on by the excitement and anxiety of seeing Leah with another man. He needs to drive a point home, and he does this quite persistently with his love spear.

He brings her to climax quickly and then manages to pull another orgasm from her before he shoots off his own load. He rests his head on her breasts, breathless, and slowly removes his cock from its warm slot. After cleaning himself up, he makes the needed adjustments to Leah's dress.

"I'm the only man for you...remember that!" he whispers and then leaves her to catch her breath. A moment later, Leah re-joins the party, but she is obviously distracted. She suddenly just

wants to get out of here.

"Can we leave?" she whispers to Manuel. He is a little confused but thinks he knows why she wants to get them alone. After making their excuses, they leave. Ray looks very pleased with herself. Karl is clearly not happy.

Back at her apartment, Manuel kisses Leah on the cheek at her front door. He turns to leave, hoping that the beautiful Leah will pull him back. She places her hand on his arm, and he turns around. The look in her eyes says everything that he wants to hear.

He finds her pussy wet and assumes that it is all him. He places his mouth on her lower lips while Leah removes her dress herself, her panties removed with Manuel's teeth already. She hopes that he will hit her spot, but he doesn't. He is very good at what he is doing, but he is certainly not Karl. Leah is determined not to judge him too hastily, however.

Then he is kissing her breasts, his tongue full on her nipples. They rise to the occasion, and he enjoys her responses to him. As he moves from breast to breast, he sends a finger into her, and then another. Soon enough he has three fingers in her, but she is well aware that he is no Karl. Still, she determines to give him a chance.

They make it to her bed, and she collapses on it, with Manuel's fingers still inside her. She needs to know what he has to offer, so she turns them around so that he can continue fingering her while she comes face to face with his dick. It is quite an impressive piece of equipment, and she is relieved.

She takes it into her mouth and finds that it tastes like lavender, probably his shower gel. She slides her lips up and down the length of his shaft, settling the head deep in the back of her throat. Manuel cannot believe the intensity of this sensation, never being deep-throated before, and she is fully aware of this from the sounds that escape his mouth. She decides to keep at it for a while, just to keep his fingers inside her. He is doing a stellar job on her cunt with his digits.

When she finally cums, Manuel is pleased with himself. He licks up her juices and then kisses her clit. She lifts her mouth off his dick and notices a trickle of pre-cum, which she hungrily laps up. Then they are facing each other, locked at the lips, tasting each other. Suddenly Leah forgets about Karl completely, and she can focus her energy on the matter at hand.

Manuel manages to bring her to another orgasm with his mouth while pulling a condom over his penis. She doesn't even know where he got it, or if he is just always prepared. His pants were in the living room, but she cannot even think of the how's of what is about to happen. She wants Manuel to fuck every trace of Karl out of her.

He does just that. They fuck for hours, Manuel moving gently in and out of her, no trace of the aggression that she had become so used to with Karl. She enjoys every second of it and has more orgasms than she can count. He also manages to cum a couple of times, making quick work of the condom changes. He is very good at this one-night stand thing, Leah realizes, and she decides not to commit to him. He will be a welcome distraction from Karl Von Helsing, however, and so she decides to keep him around if he wants to.

5

Leave Him...The text from Karl comes through as she is about to leave her house. She decides to ignore it. After all, how can he tell her not to have a lover, when he goes home to his wife every night? Fuck him, she thinks, although she cannot deny that she has developed feelings for the billionaire.

"End it!" Karl sounds anxious.

"Why?" Leah is the one who manages to be calm now.

"You know why!" Karl's arrogance translates effortlessly into the conversation.

"I'll think about it!" She hangs up

before she admits to him how he really makes her feel, already warming up just from the sound of his voice.

Leah arrives at the boutique to find Ray ogling a large bouquet of flowers. *"It's for you...I take it things went very well last night!"* She hands her the card. It isn't signed, but both of them seem to know who they're from.

"Let's just say it was interesting!" Leah is not prepared to give up any more information than she absolutely has to.

"Interesting huh?" Ray decides to leave it at that.

Leah tries hard to focus on work, she needs to really root herself in Ray's boutique and quickly become indispensable. She succeeds too, and the fact that Karl is on another trip to Europe makes it a little easier. A few more nights with Manuel, and she reckons she will soon have him out of her system.

Two weeks later, she receives a card, with an address on it, and instructions to come packed for a weekend. She assumes it is Manuel, and she is excited. She is starting to shed some of the skin that Karl had so quickly wrapped around her, and she appreciates her own resilience. She packs lightly and takes a cab to the beachfront bungalow on the address.

When she arrives, waiting with his dick in hand, is Karl Von Helsing. She doesn't even have time to question when he got back, or what explanation he will offer up to his wife, Karl already filling her mouth with his tongue, his fingers on every part of her all at the same time. Fucking Karl really is like riding a bicycle, hard to forget.

They don't speak for the two days that they are cooped up in the bungalow. Karl just reminds her over and over again of the power that he has on her, and she takes every lesson, every reminder, willingly. She thinks of Manuel once, when he calls her to confirm a date that Leah had forgotten about. She lies about being out of town and returns to fucking Karl, who really seems to think that his dick should do all the talking.

"Have you ended it?" He asks her, as he gets ready to leave on Sunday evening.

"Maybe!" She decides to play along with him if this is the only way that

she will get his attention.

"Fuck that...end it!" He leaves, no goodbye kisses, no proclamations of love.

Leah decides to wait, however, and see how things progress with Karl. If he is the jealous type, as he is proving himself to be, then that will be her trump card. She needs to protect herself anyway, for the time when he is tired of her and moves on to the next piece of ass. Manuel will be a welcome distraction from this shit, she reasons.

Sex with Karl becomes more and more intense, however. He demands more of it from her, and she starts to think that maybe, just maybe, he is falling for her, at last. She doesn't have the time to think about what this could mean for Ray, mind you. She is just enjoying this attention from this man that she now wishes she had met in a different place and time.

The lines between emotion and infatuation become blurred all the more for Leah. Karl seems to be able to control his feelings, however, and this frustrates her to no end. But then he is making love to her again, and she forgets temporarily that he is not making any declarations of love to her. She feels like she is caught in a terrible mind game, and the only winner will be Karl. She cannot resist him, however, like a moth to a flame.

"We're going to Paris for a week; I think it will help us if you come with. Karl needs to get new clothes, and we might pick up some originals for the boutique as well. Are you in?" Ray asks the question in her usual *'you will be coming with us to Paris'* fashion.

"Paris... You, me, and Mr. Von Helsing?" Leah needs to be sure that she hears correctly.

"Yes dear, have you ever been? We will have adjoining suites so that you can have your privacy but I can also have access to you when I need you. Do you have a passport?" Ray has already made up her mind that Leah will be with them in Paris. *"Karl actually suggested that I take you with, so you can buy his clothes. You just need to sleep with him now, and you will have taken my place..."* Ray makes a joke that hits a little too close to home.

Two days later, they touch down in Paris.

Lying on her bed in her part of the

double suit, Leah cannot help but think how lucky she is. Everything seems to have worked out much better than she expected, and she runs her fingers over the thousand-thread count linen, overwhelmed by the feeling that she has *arrived*. She thinks of Manuel briefly and realizes that if she can just get over her obsession with the man in the other suite, her life will be pretty damn close to perfect.

She hears noises coming from the other room, and she immediately knows what they are. She tries to drown out the noise by covering her head with the pillows, but instinctively she tries to strain to hear what Karl is doing with Ray. Eventually, she cannot resist the urge to have a look, and she goes over to the door that separates the two spaces.

She unlocks it and opens it slowly, not even sure what she is going to do when she gets into the other room. Just as the door opens, she closes it again slightly, because right there, on the large sofa in the living room area, are Karl and Ray, naked, with Ray's legs wrapped around her husband's face. She invented that move, she thinks.

Leah watches as Karl digs into his wife with his tongue, and then lick around her vagina gently. She wonders why he never approaches their lovemaking with so much care, but she assumes that she is his fantasy. There are so many differences in the way he touches her and the way she sees him touching Ray, Leah no longer sees herself as Ray's competitor for his affection. She sees herself as an accessory to this moment, and she hates it with everything in her.

She watches Karl mount her, without a condom on, and he watches her move underneath him, receiving him into her depths. Ray is apparently loving it, and Karl is enjoying being inside her. They move in tandem on one another for the longest time, and Leah is totally distraught. She cannot take this anymore, but she cannot bring herself to close the door, and to stop looking at the scene unfolding in front of her.

When the scene finally dies down, Ray is in Karl's arms, and he is stroking her up and down her arm. Leah watches his fingers move up and down her body and then finding her cunt again. She wraps her legs around his hand as he finds the inside of her with his fingers. She manages to get his cock in her mouth while he fingers her, and both Karl and Ray come to an orgasm that can only be described as beautiful.

Does he know that she is watching them? Is this part of his game, showing her what she is missing out on? What is he playing at? Or if he is not aware that she is watching them, how is it that he can separate his life with his wife and his time with her so perfectly? Leah closes the door slowly and takes these unanswered questions back to her own room.

She decides to go out and get a taste of Paris. Ray and Karl will probably be sleeping for the rest of the evening, and so she is not expecting to be needed. She goes out into the streets of Paris, completely unfamiliar territory for her, but she assumes that she cannot find it hard to get laid in the city of love. Leah doesn't even know what she is really thinking, or even what she is hoping will happen, but she just needs to get out of there.

She finds a bar nearby the hotel and goes in. Armed with a credit card, courtesy of Ray, she decides to have a drink or two, and hopefully attract the attention of one man at least. She orders a vodka on the rocks, simply because she does not have the vocabulary to order anything else. Then she waits...and waits...

Soon enough, she is surrounded by American accents and wondering how it is that she feels suddenly that she is back in New York or LA, at the local watering hole. They try to speak to her in broken French, and on a whim, she decides to pretend not to know what they're saying. They try English, and she manages to look even more confused. The last thing she wants is to be fucked by an American in Paris.

"You speak French?" The accent is thick, French, toasted, and beautiful. She turns around to see who is speaking to her.

"Not at all, no..." she replies while checking him out, sizing him up and down and liking everything that she sees. He has a dark, broody look, not unlike Manuel, and he is tall, very tall so that she is sure that he must be

packing quite a package between his legs.

She wonders how she might navigate the language barrier if this man cannot really string together many sentences in English. However, she has a feeling that language will not be necessary in the near future if she is lucky. Thankfully, however, the dark stranger, who has introduced himself as Philippe, speaks English well enough.

It takes them two hours before they are comfortable enough with one another for her to agree to get out of here. He helps her to her feet, although she is not really that drunk, and guides her out of the bar. He doesn't hail a cab, so she assumes that he must live nearby, which is a good thing she thinks, especially if she needs to make that awkward post one-night stand escape in the early hours of the morning.

She throws her eyes around the tiny fourth-floor apartment, and the first thing she realizes is how small it is. Paris is beautiful, however, so she figures that people in France just use their apartments to sleep. One thing that is large, however, is the bed. She can see it from the small entrance hall, and she cannot wait to get onto it. She is in another country, her first overseas visit, so she decides not to be embarrassed that she might be seen to be easy to this stranger she will probably never see again.

His kisses are warm, and she likes them. He undresses her slowly until she is standing naked in the darkness. Then he proceeds to kiss every inch of her while he undresses. She cannot remember feeling quite so appreciated before. The French are really very good at all things to do with lovemaking. Then they are both naked and kissing again.

Philippe lift her off the ground easily and carries her to the bed. He places her down gently, face down, and digs his fingers into the small of her back. Then he runs his fingers up the sides of her spine, and she is immediately washed with a sense of relaxation. Her legs part instinctively.

He kisses her up and down her back, and then on her buttocks, sending shivers up and down her spine. She just wants to turn over and let him take her, but she correctly reads that he wants to direct this show. Then he lifts her butt slightly, and runs his tongue over her clit, before finding her asshole with the hot flesh. She breathes deep into the pillow as she lets out a long moan, never ever having had someone's tongue on her ass before.

She is grateful that he seems to be really enjoying this because he seems to do it forever. He moves between her asshole and her cunt with his tongue until she is squirting the product of this pleasure into his mouth. Then he turns her over so that she is on her back and props himself up on his elbow, looking at her. She looks deep into his eyes and thinks of ways that she can thank him for this experience. She realizes, though that there is nothing that she can do to this man that probably has not been done to him before.

"Did you enjoy?" he asks, in a low, husky whisper.

"Yes...very much!" She tries to sound as sexy as she possibly can despite her breathlessness.

She feels the tip of his finger on her

clit again, and she is practically shaking. He runs around it a few times, in small circles, and then he finds the place where her lips separate to allow him inside her. He eases his thick finger into her so slowly that she feels like she is going to explode. She doesn't, and soon he is fingering her very, very delicately with his two thickest fingers. Leah cannot hold back from cumming again.

Then he is suddenly on top of her, easing his cock into her, carefully, because he is really packing a huge parcel. Leah has not seen it, and this was part of his plan. She might have been intimidated by its size if she saw this massive monster, and so he was quite careful not to reveal himself to her. The look on her face says that it is going to be a moment before she adjusts to his size, however.

He slowly starts to nudge his way into her, practically a millimeter at a time, until she is able to receive him entirely. Then he rests for a moment, giving her pussy time to adjust to this stretch. Then he is extracting his cock from her slowly, right before he is pushing back inside her. She lets herself go, relaxing as much as she can, and excreting as much juice from inside her vagina as possible, and soon enough, Philippe is able to thrust comfortably in and out of her tiny pussy.

Philippe fucks her for what feels like hours. In fact, the sun has started to come up over the rooftops of Paris, and he is still moving in and out of her at a consistent pace. He seems to be in no hurry to get anywhere, and she is definitely not complaining. She knows that if he was even a little bit more aggressive, he might literally have ripped her pussy to shreds. So she appreciates his consideration, and she just lets him take her in whatever way will work best for him.

Then he starts to thrust a little harder, a little faster. She really feels this stretch now, but she commits himself to taking it, letting him satisfy himself for all the satisfaction that he has allowed her to have. Another hour passes, and finally, he cums, not groaning, not grunting, just breathing very heavily. Then he kisses her lightly on her mouth for the longest time, until his penis goes slightly flaccid, allowing him to extract it easier.

"Thank you..." he whispers.

"No...no...thank you!" she responds, and then she turns over, not able to hold herself back from falling asleep.

Two hours later she is back in her hotel suite, and having a long luxurious bath. There are no messages from Ray, so she assumes that they are still asleep, or that they have gone out. She gets ready for the day, and waits for instructions from her boss, with the taste of the Frenchman still full in her mouth, and the sensation of his hands on her, and his fingers inside her, and his dick moving with slow determination in and out of her, still very present in her mind.

She makes a point of getting her fair share of Frenchmen before she gets back to LA, knowing without a shadow of a doubt that this will go a long way to getting her mind off Karl *fucking* Von Helsing...

When they arrive back in LA, Leah has a definite spring in her step. Ray notices this, and she can guess why. She also knows better than to ask her about it, however, and so she just smiles and nods at her. Leah smiles and nods back, and that is the end of that conversation. She doesn't even ask her about Manuel.

Karl is concerned, however, feeling that he has lost his grip on Leah. She has come up with excuses as to why she cannot be alone with him, and none of these explanations have anything to do with his wife. She has pictures of the clothing that they purchased in Paris, and she just sends him photos of the items that she suggests that he puts on to whatever function he has requested her help with. Now he starts to show frustration.

Leah does not let it get to her, however, focusing her energies on Manuel. They go on a couple of double dates with the Von Helsings' and Karl is clearly irritated. She really plays it up, however, and kisses Manuel openly, with extremely public displays of affection. Finally, Karl cannot take it anymore.

He makes arrangements for them to meet at a hotel again, and he is so persistent that Leah finally agrees. She gets to the hotel and meets him at the bar. After a few drinks, she decides to go up to the room. In the room, Karl starts to touch her, and she can honestly say to herself that she is not really feeling anything for him. But then he is kissing her, deeply, passionately, and without saying a word to her, he is reminding her of the effect that he knows he has on her.

She tries to fight him, knowing that she is going to let him make love to her, but trying with everything that she has not to feel anything about it. His hands are on her again, and in her, and she is melting. She hates herself for feeling the way that she is and hates the fact that even after all the sex that she has had for the last while, she still cannot believe that she is still drawn to this man.

Karl is married. He is married to her boss. He is a middle-aged German, nothing like anything that she would have thought that she would ever be attracted to. How is it that she got to this place, and how is it that she is still feeling the way that she is about him? There are no answers to these questions; at least, none that comes to mind while Karl is making love to her. And he is really making love to her right now.

When he finally finishes with her, she is overcome by the urge for some direction. She needs to know once and for all where she stands with this man, and if there is anything more than just sex that he associates with this interaction. She loves him. She realizes this, and she needs to say it to him.

"I love you..." she says eventually and looks at him with incredible anxiety and anticipation. She really needs him to say the words back to her. She cannot imagine what she will do if he doesn't, if he cannot say the words and mean them. Karl just looks at her, however, for the longest time, and then he kisses her on the side of her face. Then he gets up, and grabs his clothes, no goodbyes, no explanations, and no *'I Love You's'*... She is left wondering what the hell just happened here, and why she cannot shake the German's hold on her, no matter how hard she tries.

6

A soft knock on the hotel room door pulls Leah from the bed. She throws on a robe from the hotel's collection and goes to see who it is. It's Karl, who has just left the room with her waiting for him to tell her he loves her, but nothing. He pulls her close, and kisses her hard and deep, still not saying the words that she so desperately wants to hear.

He pushes her back into the room, taking off the clothing that he had just put on. Leah's confusion soon gives way to her other appetites, and she is helping Karl out of his trousers. If this is just sex, then, at least, it has to be good sex. She decides not to just be an accessory to these liaisons, but rather a participant.

Leah doesn't even notice when he puts the condom on, or if indeed he has, but soon enough he is inside her again. There was no foreplay, this time, no need for it. Karl enters her with such force that she gasps, making her think that he really wants her. She just has to believe this, because there is nothing else that she can allow herself to believe.

Karl thrusts forcefully inside her, and she cannot deny that she actually likes it. There are moments that she wants to be made love to, but not with Karl. She accepts that that part of him belongs to another woman, and that is okay. Theirs is to fuck the shit out of each other and have a beautiful fucking day.

Then he turns her over, and she almost expects his tongue to find her asshole. It doesn't. Instead, he is in her pussy again, from the back, his hands on her breasts, squeezing hard. She looks down at the long cock moving in and out of her, and she takes her own fingers to her clit. She will be satisfied when this is over. She just has to be.

Karl manages to get them back on the bed, Leah still face down, with his dick ramming in and out of her. He seems determined to cum, but unable to. She doesn't care, knowing that she is having multiple orgasms so that it doesn't really matter. When he finally does cum, she is so tired that she cannot even be bothered that he just leaves. She curls up on the bed and very quickly falls asleep.

She has a new verve at work now. This comes from her new realization that she is actually a beautiful woman and that she stands out from the crowd. She also happens to be very good at what she does, even though she is not a stylist in any sort of official capacity. She does not even try to avoid Karl anymore, even though the reasons for this are mostly selfish.

The fact that Karl cannot say that he loves her does bother her, however. She is not going to let this get to her, though. So what if he cannot commit to her with words. At least, he cannot keep his hardness from inside her, and that is a good place to start, she reckons. She will remain open to other relationships, however, and other sexual encounters. One day, when she has worked through how she feels for Karl, she reckons that there will come a day when she doesn't need to please him anymore.

Ray wonders about her relationship with Manuel however, since Leah has not mentioned him in quite a while. She tries to juggle her busy schedule with finding another suitor for young Leah. According to her, Leah is too beautiful to be single. She correctly assumes that she is single again, but she does not press Leah for the details of the breakup.

She watches Leah at work, aggressively throwing herself into everything that she is tasked to do. This commitment to work seems manic, even for workaholic Ray, who is also incredibly busy with work. She decides to consult her trusted black book, especially since Karl seems to have no interest in hooking Leah up with one of his associates.

"So, is Leah seeing anyone?" Tristan Mills, a rock star newbie client of hers wants to know. Ray sees an opportunity here.

"No, actually...she is very single!" Ray already has their first meeting planned in her head before Tristan even confirms that he is, in fact, interested in Leah.

"Do you have a rule about your staff dating your clients?" he asks Ray, almost expecting to be shot down.

"Tristan, honey...this is LA...Everybody sleeps with everybody!" This is not the response that Tristan expected from Ray, and he is immediately relaxed.

"So, how do I get her number?" he asks, rather shyly.

"Well, I can do one better...Leah?" She calls Leah into her office and introduces the two of them. She isn't sure if Leah is just being nice, or if she is humoring her, so she goes quickly in for the kill. *"Tristan is new in town, and I thought that you could show him a few of the hangouts, courtesy of our credit card, of course!"* Ray is telling her to take him out, and she knows that she cannot say no.

"Sure...When?" Leah asks, slightly annoyed, but not showing it.

"Tonight! Go home and get ready, and meet Tristan at his hotel, the

Beverly Hills right?"

"*Right...*" Tristan makes his goodbyes and goes off to get ready too, after thanking Ray of course, and after walking Leah out of the boutique and getting her a cab.

Tristan cleans up pretty good, and Leah is forced to accept that Ray is actually very good at what she does. He doesn't look a thing like the heavy metal rocker that she met in Ray's office earlier. He has black jeans and a black shirt on, and except for his tattoos, and earrings, you would assume that he was a doctor or an investment banker.

She is thankful that she decided to wear a short cocktail dress that she got in Paris, a dark brown number that suits her complexion so much she looks like the chocolate dip on a fondue fountain. They look good together too, Leah catching their reflection in the large foyer mirror in the hotel.

Thankfully, Tristan seems to have more than music on the brain, and the conversation flows smoothly. Leah times her drinks perfectly, however so that she doesn't lose her inhibitions too quickly. Tristan, on the other hand, drinks rather quickly. However, there are no noticeable changes in his behavior, much to Leah's relief.

They move from one club to another and then choose a quiet bar on the popular Rodeo Drive. Leah senses that she is not really needed as a chaperone, but she needed to get out too, so she is not complaining. Also, there is no need for her to bring out the credit card that she is armed with, the couple getting special treatment at every venue that they go to, and Tristan insisting on paying for their dinner and drinks.

Tristan drops her off at her apartment and then leaves once she is safe in the building. She is impressed with his restraint, and she almost wraps herself on the knuckles for deciding earlier in the evening that she would sleep with him that night. After a quick shower, she jumps into bed alone and strangely excited. There's just something about Tristan!

She realizes the next day what it is about Tristan that excites her. She has made it to page three of the local tabloids, with a series of question marks above her picture. This means that she is going to quickly, become a celebrity, even if it is just for the fact that she is thought to be dating one. Manuel was great, but they never went out in public. He was far too concerned with his image. Tristan not so much.

Leah knows that it is only a matter of time before Karl learns of this new relationship. She cannot wait, and so she decides to fast track this, accepting every date that Tristan makes, ensuring that they are very visible. Even though Tristan has made no attempts to sleep with her yet, she is sure to place careful public displays of affection that give the illusion of a rather robust sex life.

She knows why she wants to rub Karl up the wrong way. This is the only way that she seems to be able to get his attention. This is the only time that he gives some indication of wanting her affections exclusively. She is willing to take what she can get, even if it is just Karl's juvenile *'nobody plays with my toys'* tantrums.

After a few weeks, however, Leah has received no contact from Karl. Maybe he has moved on. Maybe he just doesn't care anymore. She doesn't know, and she tries to convince herself that she doesn't care. She decides to be the aggressor and to really sleep with Tristan. He has waited too long to make a move, and there is no reason why she cannot be so bold.

She decides to invite Tristan to her apartment for a private dinner. To her surprise, he tries to get out of it, suggesting that they try out the new Cuban place near Malibu. Leah is determined, however, and offers to cook him a nice Cuban dinner if that's what he really wants. Eventually, after much convincing, he agrees, offering to bring the wine.

He arrives at her apartment a little after seven, armed with two bottles of wine, and a flustered look on his face. She puts it off to his busy schedule and pours him a drink. Then she busies herself in her open plan kitchen while Tristan makes a mess of chopping up some vegetables. She manages to salvage them, however, and in about thirty minutes, dinner is served.

They eat and chat easily. She is surprised by how comfortable she is with him also. After dinner, they open the second bottle of wine and relax on the sofa. She places her hand on his leg and watches his face. She cannot deny the slight flinch that she notices on his face so that she eventually has to ask him.

"Is everything okay?"

"Yes, sure!"

"Then why do I get the impression that you do not want me to touch you?"

"No... you are extremely attractive!"

"Then why don't you come and show me just how attractive I am!"

"Uhm, there's something that I need to tell you!" Tristan really seems to be worried about something, and this is something really big.

"What is it?" Leah really wants to know!

"I'm not...very...big!" He really seems embarrassed by this. Leah suddenly remembers everything that she heard about white men, and she thinks of the ones that she has been with over the last while. There is nothing wrong with their size.

"That doesn't matter to me!"

"Seriously?"

"Yes, there is nothing for you to worry

about...I promise!" Leah is already undoing his belt buckle. She really needs to see what exactly it is that has Tristan so vexed.

Tristan stands up and lets her take his trousers off completely. He takes his shoes off and manages to get his jeans off completely. She goes for his underwear, and pulls it down slowly, anxious herself now of what she might find underneath them.

She looks up at him and smiles a reassuring smile. What hangs in front of her is a perfectly acceptable nine inches. Tristan is probably hung up on all the urban myths he has heard about black cock so that he is self-conscious about his package. He really has nothing to worry about, though. She takes his head between her lips to show him just how little concern she has for his size.

He watches his dick disappearing between Leah's lips, the excitement of acceptance adding another inch to his length. There is something to be said about being with a woman who accepts you as you are. Soon enough, Tristan is thrusting gently into her mouth, filling it completely, hitting the back of her throat. She is, at least, a little impressed; she cannot deny this.

Leah keeps his dick in her mouth while she works on her own clothing, and then on her underwear. Tristan is enjoying the view so much that it doesn't even cross his mind to help her out. Instead, he takes off his own shirt and starts pulling on his own nipples. He exhales loudly, mostly relief.

Then she stands up and leads him to the bedroom. She lays him out on the bed, going down on him again while she reaches for her emergency pack of condoms in the side dresser. She removes one from its casing, and then after treating Tristan's cock to some tongue action; she slides the condom down his firm shaft. Whatever he might lack in length he more than makes up for in girth.

Leah straddles him, sensing correctly that he is not confident enough to try and please her yet. He really let the horror stories of black stallions get to him so that he has denied himself all the sex that his looks would have allowed him. She is almost pleased, happy to be giving him one of his first full experiences. Leah rides him to a quick climax, and when he doesn't lose his erection, she takes him on another trip down the garden path.

With his confidence restored somewhat, he takes her and puts her on her back. He recovers his dick and settles his cock inside her from above. There are few things in life that are more beautiful to watch than a confident man with a woman. Tristan is becoming more and more beautiful to watch. He has four orgasms before he brings Leah to her first one, but one is all she needs.

They open another bottle of wine from Leah's fridge, and lie in bed naked, drinking, and talking until the both fall asleep. The next day is the first day that Leah is late for work. Ray doesn't seem to mind, not at all in fact. Still, though, Leah is not prepared to go into too much detail about her tryst. Ray too, seems to have run out of things to say about her and Karl's bedroom activity.

"*You're getting very popular,*" Ray says to her a few days later.

"*Why?*" Leah asks, taking the card that Ray is holding out to her.

It's from another client, an African-American actor named Chris, middle-aged, single. She is flattered, but not really interested. Just how many men can one woman date at the same time? And, truth be told, she is still focused on Karl, who has yet to confront her about her new relationship. It won't be long now, though; she tells herself.

She finds herself suddenly overwhelmed. Tristan is treating her well, but she wants Karl. Chris is also persistently pursuing her, so that she is even more confused, not sure if she should just give the brother a chance and be done with it. She really feels like she is now caught between three men, but wanting only one. How did this become her life?

Leah decides to take a few days off work. She needs to make sense of her situation and decide finally, what she is going to do. She needs to weigh in on the options in front of her and make the best decision for her. Ray is getting busy, though, and she wonders if she will be able to get away.

"I was thinking of taking a few days off...to figure things out!" Leah starts the conversation even though she

thinks she already knows how it will end.

"Trouble in paradise?" Ray asks, genuinely concerned. She is, after all, the reason that Leah is seeing Tristan in the first place.

"You could say that...I really need some space to think about...things!" Leah doesn't want to lay out what is actually bothering her, at the risk of sounding juvenile.

"Well, we have a beach house in Santa Barbara that I haven't checked on in a while. You could go and make sure everything is still there. Consider it a paid weekend away!" Ray really has a wonderful way of killing two birds with one stone, and making you feel like she was giving you what you asked for while in fact she was making you do what she wanted.

"Really...that would be great...I mean... Sure...Yes!" Leah is suddenly excited by the thought; a weekend spent in a luxurious Santa Barbara beach house might be just what she needs. And she will be paid for her *'trouble'*, which is a definite added bonus. She decides to leave this weekend, really needing the escape and

wanting just to be gone from here.

The place is beautiful, smaller than the Von Helsing's Beverly Hills mansion, but definitely more beautiful. Probably its simplicity that is so appealing. Leah really thinks that she could get used to living like this. She imagines having a place like this, all to herself, all on her own steam, and she resolves to work hard to make it happen.

She puts the champagne that she brought in the fridge and some of the food. She makes a quick inspection of the place and makes a note of everything that she sees. Leah even takes out her cell phone and takes pictures of some of the items that seem to be expensive, just so that she can send them to Ray, to confirm to her that all her valuables are still in the house.

Leah decides to take a bath. She falls asleep twice in the huge tub, waking up when the water cools down enough to shake her from her dreams. She starts to wrinkle, so that she eventually gets out of the bath, and wraps herself in a bath sheet. She goes to the fridge and pours herself some champagne, which is quite chilled now, and she makes her way onto the terrace. The sea breeze blowing in from the ocean hits her face, and she breathes it in, really feeling like things are working out for her.

There is a noise near the front door, and she turns to see what it is. She is alone, and the nearest house is a quarter mile away. She wonders if she locked it, sure that she did, but still she must go and see who it is. She almost drops her glass when she sees Karl Von Helsing standing in the entrance hall.

7

Karl is obviously drunk. She notices this because she has seen him drink before, often, but never ever seen him drunk. He stands in the entrance hall, looking at her. Leah pulls her robe over her breasts instinctively, not sure what Karl is doing here.

"So, Tristan..." Karl begins immediately with his confrontation, letting Leah know that he has come to confront her about her relationship.

"What about him?" She needs him to articulate what exactly his problem is with Tristan, just so that he can give her some semblance of an emotional attachment to her.

"I've seen the papers!" He lets her know that he has seen the public documentary of the relationship. His tone lets her know that he is not impressed with this at all.

"I see... What I don't see is what the problem is!" Leah still needs to push him for something more. She is tired of reading between the lines with Karl, even though she reads him rather accurately.

Karl walks to where the bar should be fully stocked. He finds it empty since they have not been to this particular property in about three or four months.

"Is there anything to drink?" He throws his eyes around the space as though a bottle of something might just magically appear out of nowhere.

Leah goes to the fridge and takes out the bottle of champagne, pouring Karl a glass, refilling hers. She watches him drink from the glass in what seems like a single gulp and then handing it to her for a refill. She takes the glass from him and empties the bottle into it. After handing it back to him, she turns around and takes her own drink to the terrace.

"What are you doing here Karl?" she asks him when he finally makes it onto the terrace and comes up next to her.

"I need you to stop seeing him... it's embarrassing!" He gets to the point, and Leah is reminded of how Ray also has a way of telling you what to do while of course disguising it as a request.

"And you...will you leave your wife?" She needs to meet him where he's at, and she also needs to know once and for all what he wants from her, and what he expects from her. She cannot seriously be expected to be happy with just being his *mistress* exclusively while he continues to maintain the life he has built with Ray.

"That is not even an option... Don't be naïve!" He says this as though he really expects her to be happy just being *the other woman* until he has had his fill of her.

"I'm not naïve...far from it actually. That is why I will not end it with Tristan. I need to build a life for myself that isn't attached to an already

attached man. Just how little do you think I think of myself? Clearly you don't see me! But that is now your problem, I'm afraid!" She does not believe the words she is saying, but she just feels the need for him to hear the words so that he can give her direction.

Karl is taken aback. He really has no response for this Leah, this woman who seems to have very quickly come into her own. He does not know how to respond to this self-assured young woman who has grown in leaps and bounds from the almost timid young woman he met that first day in his house.

"So we seem to be at a stalemate?" Leah presses Karl for more of a response.

"Look, Leah, I am not good with words... I am ruthless in business, and when I want something, I go for it... and I want you!"

"Well, you cannot have me exclusively... not given your own situation. That just isn't fair!" Leah feels like she might start crying, but she manages to restrain herself.

"Can you at least not flaunt your relationship in my face then...please...I

cannot handle seeing you like that with another man!" He lets her know how he feels but still does not say the words that she wants to hear from him. Again, she is reading between the lines, finding in his unspoken words everything that she wants him to say.

Leah is tired, and she doesn't want to fight with Karl. It's pointless anyway because he seems to know just what to say to allay all her concerns and leave her wanting him even more. He is obviously not going to leave his wife. He also cannot bring himself to admit that he has any real feelings for her. However, his actions really speak louder for her than any words can, and she decides to let it go, for now. She wishes that he will also just go, the feeling of confusion overwhelming her slightly.

Karl downs the second glass of champagne and puts the glass down. He walks over to Leah and takes her drink from her. He takes an enormous sip from it and then pours the remainder of the bubbles down her throat. After putting down the glass, he cups her face in his hands and pulls her face towards his. His lips are cool from the champagne, but she is instantly hot in every part of her.

His tongue finds hers, and it is immediately intense. She cannot even pull away from him. She doesn't want to. Then her tongue is in his mouth, and the heat intensifies. Their lips do not part for a second, exchanging tongues for the longest time, sucking the flavor off of each other until they are left feeling quite dry. Then their mouths produce more saliva, and they make exchanges of this oral fluid until their tongues are rehydrated. Leah feels like she can kiss Karl forever.

Karl frees Leah of her robe until she is standing naked on the terrace, the wind on her back. The breeze seems to hug her all over, and her nipples become rock hard. He takes one of them in his mouth and sucks on it hard. Then he takes the other one between his teeth, running his tongue in a flicking motion over the nipple. She cannot help but shudder, and she hates herself for responding so quickly to being touched by Karl.

His mouth warms up quickly, and this warmth transfers almost instantly to her nipples and then to her breasts.

Leah's chest warms up rapidly, and this heat moves quickly down to her belly. Her back is cool, however, and this contrast in temperature confuses her between her legs so that her clit retracts and her lips close. Her cunt, however, is on fire deep inside, and Leah wants Karl to touch her there.

Karl moves his lips down the center of her chest and reaches her belly button. He places his tongue into the groove there and proceeds to French kiss her naval. His hands find her breasts, and he pulls hard on her nipples with his fingers. This *Bermuda Triangle* of intensity sends waves up and down her legs so that she has to concentrate on keeping herself on her feet. Her knees are becoming *Jell-O* however so that she has to prop herself up on the balustrade with her hands.

Then his hands are on her waist. His tongue is out of her naval now, and he is planting soft kisses all over her belly. He parts her legs with his face and blows warm air from his mouth onto the soft curls between her legs. Her clit starts to respond, engorging so that it cannot hide itself anymore. Karl cannot resist placing his tongue on this bulging flesh, and licking it gently at first, and then more aggressively.

Then he sends his tongue between her lips and uses the tip of his fleshy tongue to part them, reaching inside her with just the first part of it, and then licking her lips so that they open up now naturally. He continues to lick the outside of her pussy, warming it up so much that she starts to ooze juices quickly. Then he uses his lips on her lips for a while, before returning to her clit with his tongue.

He holds her firmer on her hips, his hands reaching far behind her so that he has his fingers on her ass. Leah parts her legs even more now herself, wanting him to get inside her deeply. Karl sees this invitation and starts to enter her pussy with his tongue. He goes all the way up inside her and laps up the liquid on the walls of her vagina. The beating in her pussy is now relentless, but he seems to find her rhythm, and as she beats, he compliments her beating with savage licks.

Karl's phone suddenly starts to ring, and he reaches for it in his pocket. It's Ray, and he doesn't even look to see that Leah has noticed this. He continues licking the inside of her pussy for a moment and then slowly pulls out his tongue. He comes up to standing, clearing his throat, and then kisses Leah on the mouth. Then he answers his phone, nothing about his tone suggesting in the least what he was just doing.

He proceeds to have a long conversation with his wife. She can apparently hear that he is drunk, and so he doesn't deny it. He feeds her some lie about having one too many after his golf game, and going straight to his room. Leah wonders where in the world Ray thinks her husband is. She starts to walk away from this conversation that she really doesn't want to hear, but Karl will not have it.

He leans on her so that he pins her against the balustrade. He takes his free hand and puts it between her legs. After feeling around for a moment, he sends his index finger into her. She almost screams with pleasure, but she reminds herself about the conversation that she is no part of. This starts to feel like a weird threesome; Leah feeling like Ray can see her husband's finger moving around inside her. If it didn't feel so fucking good, she might have forcefully evicted him.

The conversation really seems to go on forever, and Karl is soon forcing a second finger inside her. The conversation that she cannot help listening to soon fades out into the distance as she focuses on the stretch in her pussy. She decides to concentrate on her own orgasm, leaving Karl to his multitasking, which he is doing very well indeed.

He manages to insert a third finger into her tiny slot. She holds his hand to control the penetration, the stretch proving a little too much too soon. She holds his hand tightly, but Karl seems determined to fill her pussy with his digits. Resistance is proving futile, and soon enough she has three of Karl's thick fingers easing in and out of her, stretching her cunt almost to capacity.

She is close to climax, and she digs her fingers into the balustrade. Her knuckles seem close to cracking as she borders on a massive orgasm. Just then Karl stops moving his fingers, and she can breathe. This doesn't last long, however, and soon enough he is working his way deeper inside her. She isn't even sure how many fingers are moving inside her now, but it doesn't matter. Leah is about to explode.

Leah arches her back, forcing more of the hand that is struggling now to find a hold on her cunt into it. Karl catches his breath, which sounds like a hiccup, so Ray is not suspicious. He looks up at Leah's pussy, surprised to find that he is stuffing her with four of his fingers so that he stops moving his hand. Leah wants him inside her, however, and she practically sits on his hand now.

Karl carefully works his hand around inside her now and draws more fluid from her cunt. Soon he is moving easier in and out of her, and she is headed on a collision course with her orgasm again. She starts to gasp loudly so that Karl feels the urge to end his conversation with Ray. He makes the transition effortlessly back to his chat with his wife and then says the words that Leah longs for him to say to her. *I love you* falls easily from his lips now, and he ends the sentence with his wife's name. Leah is more than a little devastated.

She focuses solely on her climax now and holds Karl's hand at the wrist. She moves his hand around in herself for herself and brings herself closer to the edge. She is soon on the path that will see her collide directly with her own pleasure, and she concentrates hard. She has to focus so that her mind does not shift to the last words she heard come out of Karl's mouth. She holds his hand steady now and grinds her groin persistently over the fingers that have made her pussy their home. She exhales hard as she comes to an incredible climax resulting in her juices all the way down Karl's forearm.

Leah releases his hand and lifts herself off it. She picks up the robe on the floor and pulls it over herself. She has no words to say to Karl, and she walks back into the house. She goes straight to the fridge and opens another bottle of champagne. She wants to drink straight from the bottle but does not want Karl to see that she has come undone. She takes another glass from the cupboard and fills it. Leah now takes a large gulp from the glass, so that it is half-full when she is done.

She goes over to the living area and turns the TV on. She needs anything to distract her from what has just happened. She hates herself for letting Karl bring her to climax, but she just could not help it. He just makes her feel so damn good. He knows how to touch her, where to touch her. Karl seems to read all her signals, and she has to admit to herself that she really likes it.

She cannot, however, handle the mixed signals anymore. She makes a commitment to herself to make everything with Karl about the sex going forward. It is going to be hard, she knows it, but she has no choice. Leah has to try, though, and she commits herself to making this work for herself at least. Karl obviously has one thing on his mind, and he sees her as just a piece of meat. Exclusive meat yes, but meat nonetheless, he sees her as his own personal prized possession.

Karl seems oblivious to her feelings really, and he has his tongue on her pussy again. She really doesn't feel like having sex with Karl, not tonight anymore at least, however, she knows that he won't take no for an answer. He has his tongue firmly placed inside her cunt, and she is impressed by this skill given his current state. He even remembers a condom and wraps it firmly on his rock hard cock.

There is no time for her to think too much now, as Karl mounts her on the couch. He goes deep, and he goes hard. She knows that any chance of restraint went out of the window with his tenth drink. The champagne that he has had here hasn't helped either. Leah adjusts herself underneath his insistent thrusting and finds a place where she is comfortable. Then she lets him ride her all the way to the finish.

Karl takes an incredibly long time to cum, and in this time, Leah can focus on nothing but the massive cock inside her. He seems to have grown a couple of inches, but she knows that this is just a result of the position that she is in. She tries to resist holding him, but cannot. Eventually, she is pulling him deeper into her, and he is resting so far inside her that she feels he might push the back walls of her cunt down completely.

It lasts for hours, and Leah cannot stop herself from having multiple orgasms. She is exhausted by the time Karl finally explodes, and she just leaves him there to lie in her arms, half passed out, half not. His dick remains rock hard, however, and this forces Leah to stay pinned to the couch, with Karl thrusting slowly, but not. There are moments when she wants to get him off her, but she is enjoying the fullness of the meat inside her, so she stays just where she is.

8

"*I want to fuck you...*" Karl says on the phone a few days after she gets back to Beverly Hills.

"*Go on...*" Leah gets up and leaves the office where Ray is busy with paperwork, but it seems that she can hear the voice on the other end belongs to her husband.

"*I'm thinking...*" Karl appears to want to ask her something that he isn't sure she will agree to.

"Yes?" Leah starts to get a little nervous.

"*I'll bet we could fuck on the roof of the Hyatt before anybody finds us!*" She wouldn't have expected Karl to be so adventurous; she knows she definitely isn't.

"What?" Leah has no idea how she is going to say no to Karl's request.

"I'm serious!" Karl really is, and Leah knows this, somehow.

"I know... and no!" She hopes that this is all that she needs to say to dissuade him from this bizarre request. Fortunately, Ray needs her for something and so she has to hang up the call. She cannot help but wonder what this new side to Karl is, or where it comes from. She thinks of the effect that fucking her has had on Ray's sex life. Leah wonders who it is that is fucking Karl now. She wonders who is introducing him to this new measure of kink.

About ten minutes later, Karl calls again, Ray this time. After about three minutes, she hangs up. Then she looks at Leah, and squints. She knows that what she is about to ask her is over and above the call of duty, but she is going to ask her anyway.

"My husband needs you..." Ray says, looking at her watch, seeing that it is already after four.

"For?" Leah asks, half choking.

"An event tonight...He needs you to style him; he'll pick you up in ten minutes!" Here we go again with her orders disguised as requests.

Leah packs up her desk almost immediately and feels slightly annoyed that Karl went over her head just to get her alone. She hopes that he really needs her to dress him, and this is not going to be a one-way trip to the rooftop of the Hyatt. A moment later Karl is outside and calling the boutique for Leah to come out.

Leah is quiet in the car all the way to the mansion. Karl pulls up in front of the garage after slowly driving up the long driveway, looking at Leah throughout. She is suddenly edgy and uncomfortable, and she wishes that she had decided to wear a longer dress or jeans. Her thighs are exposed, and Karl's eyes now rest comfortably on them.

Leah is suddenly aware of all the sounds of the garden. Even the gate that is humming shut at the bottom of the driveway sounds like it is shutting in her ears. She is far too alert for what Karl apparently wants to do to her, and she opens the door. Karl stops her with a firm hand on her thigh. She throws him a *'don't you dare'* look.

"*I really want to fuck you...*" He whispers, almost breathlessly.

"*Not here...*" she says. Leah tries to get out of the car again.

Karl reclines the seat that she is sitting on, and she falls back, her seatbelt still on so that there is no way for her to escape his hold. He lifts her dress and kisses her cunt over the soft fabric of her panties. Then he exposes the soft curls covering her pussy and settles his nose in them, and then he is licking her wet so that she is not sure if the moisture is coming from inside her or not.

He is very quick about getting his own seatbelt undone, and she is looking at him with a few questions in her eyes. She doesn't understand where this is coming from and why he cannot wait at least until they are inside. The next moment he is inside her with his cock so that she is not sure what is going on. There is no place for her legs to move. There is no space for him except for the space that he has created for himself between her legs with his dick. Leah is not sure what is going one here, so that she has her hands up above her ears and she looks out of the dark windows of the car, straining to see outside the almost black tint.

She is almost not present at the moment, and when she notices headlights pulling up behind them, she is suddenly still. This cannot be happening; she thinks to herself, Ray pulling up behind them. She hadn't realized that it was getting dark outside, and she hopes that Ray doesn't look into the car. She tries to draw Karl's attention to the problem that they have, and yet Karl is just thrusting into her, no concern for anything that is going on around them.

She tries to silence herself, and she bites into Karl's shoulder. He seems to enjoy the thrill, assured that even if Ray could look into the car, there is no way that she could see into the car. He moves his butt, using this muscle, and only this muscle, to thrust his cock deeper into Leah. She really bites down hard into the flesh of his shoulder now, and she is trying hard to see whether Ray passes the car.

The window goes darker for a split second, and then the shadow is gone. Ray is on the phone, and she is just making it to the front door. Leah wants Karl to be finished inside her, and she intends to be out of here. After a few more solid thrusts, he exhales hard, and he is done. Again she does not cum; she does not want to. This is incredibly risky, and she cannot imagine going inside and facing Ray.

There is a moment when she wants him to make her cum, but she cannot even think about that right now. She pushes him off her and after a brief resistance, Karl takes his cock out of Leah's warm place. He takes care of the condom while she covers herself up, insisting that he doesn't need to make her cum. They need to reach some kind of consensus about what they are going to do now, how they are going to get into the house, and where they are going to say they have been.

"We are going to have to go in...she's obviously seen my car." Karl states the obvious.

"No, you have to go in. I'm leaving. I'll call a cab from the street!" Leah really just wants to be out of here.

"Don't be silly, what about my look?" Karl seems to enjoy this new game that he is playing. *"Besides, we can just say that I was showing you the garden. You haven't seen it yet, have you?"*

"Fine...fine...Let's just go!" Leah really just wants to get out of the car, and after checking her reflection in the mirror, she gets out of the car. She is careful about closing the car door softly, but the chances of Ray hearing the door slam shut from inside the house are really minimal.

They go around the back of the house and up the back terrace stairs. Leah still feels like she is looking less than put together, and she is right. She is looking a little out of sorts, and so she is forcing herself to try and pull herself together. There is no time for her to sort herself out anymore, though, because they turn into to living room to find Ray having a drink, looking out of the window.

"Oh...where have you two been?" She asks, just for the sake of, a million other things on her mind.

"Leah wanted to see the garden!" Karl says, matter-of-factly, and then plants a long, passionate kiss on his

wife's lips. *"Shall we go upstairs and sort out my look, before I'm late?"* He is speaking to both Ray and Leah so that they both follow him upstairs to his dressing room. A half an hour later, Karl is ready for his night out, and he leaves Leah to have a drink with his wife before her cab gets here.

Back in her apartment, Leah thinks of how calm Karl was in his house, and the ease with which he kissed his wife. Surely, some taste of her must have been left on his lips, in his mouth. She has to stop wondering all these things and has to let go of the fact that she wants Karl to love her. He is obviously in love with his wife, and there is really nothing that she can do about that.

The next Saturday she is working with Ray at her house. Karl is thankfully not here, and so Leah can focus on work. She gets through quite a bit, so that by the time he does return, she is almost ready to go home. There is just one more thing that Ray needs her to do, but her husband needs to steal her away for a moment.

Ray and Karl go into the sunroom, Karl kissing her before she has a chance to close the door. He actually seems to be on heat, but Ray is somewhat conservative, and with Leah in the next room, she finds it inappropriate that she is in this room kissing her husband. Karl has a way of making everything okay, however, and he has a way of making you overlook protocol, and just be. She has no idea what Karl really wants her to do, or how far he is going to go with this, but he is making his intentions very clear.

Leah stands by the door, unable to resist the urge to see what they are about to do. He has his lips on her neck, and so Leah takes a hand to her own neck, running her fingers down the parts on Ray that Karl is enjoying. Ray is, fortunately, facing away from the door, but Karl is looking directly at her, and this is a strange feeling, even for her. What is Karl playing at here?

She watches as he removes his cock from his trousers, Leah's eyes falling on this part of his anatomy. Karl strokes his meat, moving his hand up and down his shaft, almost willing her to come in and touch it. She wants to, however, but she realizes the weirdness of this situation. There is nothing that she can do about the penis that is so close to her; she could reach out and touch it. She knows that she needs to turn away from the door. She cannot move, however.

"Karl, we can't!" Ray says, turning her head to look at the door. Karl quickly moves her face back towards his, and he kisses her deeply.

"Of course we can. I need to leave in a minute, and I won't see you for a whole two days. Let me have my fill honey, please!" He is insistent, something that Leah has to admit to herself she finds quite attractive. This is probably the most attractive thing about Karl, actually, she thinks.

He exposes her breasts, promising to be done really quickly. He also promises her that he will not leave until she is also completely satisfied. Her dress drops to her ankles, and then her panties follow. She is not wearing a bra, totally unnecessary thanks to a recent boob job. Leah looks at her perfect breasts, and she cannot help but compare them to her own.

Karl sends a finger into his wife, feeling for the wetness that will allow him ease of access. She is still a little too dry, and so he moves his finger around inside her, drawing moisture from deep inside his wife, until at last, she starts to ooze liquid from her depths. He throws his eyes at the door again, meeting Leah's eyes, and holding her gaze while he holds onto the inside of his wife.

Then he is entering her, and for a moment, his eyes close. Leah feels a tug in her own belly, not arousal, but jealousy. She never thought of herself as jealous until just now. She hates this feeling. She wishes that she could rip it out of her, but she can't. Yet still, Leah cannot pull her eyes away from the scene playing out in front of her.

As Karl begins to thrust into his wife, she feels like her heart is being wrenched out of her chest. This is a very new emotion for her, and she doesn't know what to do with it. He moves inside Ray with a tenderness that he has never shown to her. There are moments where she cannot believe the difference between the way he touches her and the way he is now touching Ray. She remembers the way he was with her in Paris, and she suddenly knows her real place in his life.

Still, she cannot pull herself away from the sunroom door. There is just a part of her that needs to see the end of this scenario. Then she hears him tell his wife *he loves her*, and there is no escaping the sound of every syllable: "*I love you, Ray*" ... he says! Again, she is torn.

9

"**D**id you enjoy the show?" Karl sends Leah a text the next day. She decides to ignore it, still needing an explanation for the reasons why he made love to his wife. This is absurd; she knows since he owes her no such thing. He insists on antagonizing her. However, he seems to be the one drawing reactions from her now.

Karl doesn't apologize for making love to his wife, why should he. Leah needs to learn her place in the affair, or he might be forced to end it. He still sees a use for her, however, and her delicious pussy, so he hopes it will not come to that. She really does need to relax, though, or he might lose this pussy that is so different from his wife's, and so eager to please him.

Leah has her own reasons for believing the shit that Karl tells her. She reads his texts over and over again; they are coming in fast and steady, and she sees in his words what she wants to see. The last text is a request for her to style him for an event, a corporate dinner. She has not responded to any texts so far, and she considers ignoring this one too. Instead, after deleting every other text, she shows it to Ray.

Ray doesn't even bat an eyelid. Instead, she offers Leah a ride to her own house after lunch; then she can take the rest of the afternoon off. Leah almost appreciates the fact that Ray will be at the house too, meaning that Karl will not be able to have his way with her. She needs a break from him and his dick, just to build the desire again. She doesn't know how to play him anymore, and she needs a moment to regroup.

The three of them are in Karl's dressing room. Leah is in professional mode, and she busies herself with some clothing items while Ray and Karl kiss and converse in the corner. She has made peace with this situation, although she does notice that Karl is a little bit thrown by Ray's presence in the house. He makes the shift quickly, however, and when he asks for Ray's opinion on the looks that Leah puts in front of him, starts to feel more and more like an addendum.

Leah turns away as Karl puts on his trousers, and then she turns to face him to make the necessary adjustments. She is careful about letting her hands linger too long on Karl, even though Karl is practically pushing his soft cock into her fingers at every opportunity. She really just wants to reach out and touch him, but she cannot. Ray jokes about having another woman's hands on her husband, and then she kisses him passionately.

Karl seems to thrive on this thrill, and his dick begins to go hard. Leah again turns her eyes away from him, Karl seeming oblivious to this *growing* problem. Ray kisses him once more and then instructs Leah to come down and say goodbye before she leaves. She has a phone call to make, and so she excuses herself. Karl is quick to seize the opportunity.

He whips out his cock quickly and pulls her to him. He pushes her down on his penis and rubs it across her closed mouth. For a moment, she doesn't know what to do, and then she parts her lips. He quickly takes the gap and pushes his meat onto her warm tongue. She cannot help herself, and soon enough she is sucking on his hardening manhood. Karl very quickly sports a massive erection.

Leah closes her eyes so that she does not see Ray if she happens to come into the room. She knows that she cannot stop herself now, and she is really giving Karl's dick the most incredible oral action he has seen in a while. There is no time for anything else, they both know this, so both of them really just give themselves completely to this moment, this one act.

She holds his dick firmly in her hands now, needing to keep it steady so that she can work on it with her lips and her tongue. She hopes that he will cum quickly, but he is giving no indication either way, and so she increases the pressure up and down his shaft. He eventually starts to moan, so that she knows that she is finally having an effect on him.

She gains momentum, and keeps it, knowing that there is no time for her to get creative with this. He needs to cum, and she needs this connection with his dick, to satisfy places in herself that she cannot deny. She sucks hard on his head, and then up and down his shaft until his cock starts to pulsate, as does her pussy. She wants to reach down and touch herself, but she has already got Karl so close now that there is not turning back.

Karl starts to cum in her mouth, and she keeps on sucking and swallowing, just to make sure that none of his cum escapes her mouth. Soon enough she has milked his meat completely with her mouth, and she kisses the head tenderly with her lips. She pulls her hair out of her face and stands up, as Karl puts himself away. She is the one to leave the room first, this time, needing a drink to wash the taste of Karl's seed out of her mouth.

She gets downstairs and sees Ray on her laptop. Leah hopes that her boss will offer her a drink, and so she just hangs around for a minute. She is just about to say her goodbyes when Ray finally comes up from her laptop and says the words she longs to hear. The martini pitcher has already been on her radar, and she watches greedily as Ray pours her a glass. She has to pace herself so that she does not swig the whole glass down, and she manages to sip steadily and rinse some of the semen out of her mouth and down her throat.

Leah makes her escape as Karl starts to come down the stairs. She calls the cab as she walks out of the front door, and by the time she makes it to the gate, she has to wait for Ray to open the gate. Soon enough she is on the other side of the gate, after she calls Ray to let her out, and then she walks down the road a little bit, needing to just be away from the house.

The cab pulls up next to her, and she gets in. She guesses from his accent that he is probably from the Ukraine, but she has no references to this assumption. What she knows for sure is that he is a man, and he is a rather handsome man, and she has an itch thanks to Karl Von Helsing, an itch that she is hoping this man might be enticed to scratch for her.

She checks his fingers as he grips the steering wheel. They are long and thick, and there is no tell-tale sign of a wedding ring. She hopes that he is open to suggestion, but caution demands that she doesn't take him back to her place. Her eyes dart around wildly for a dark alley that she can make her suggestion in.

Leah thinks of Tristan, and she considers calling him. He is out of town, however, and so she knows that this will not work. She makes a move, lifting her dress high, and crossing her legs, hoping that he is checking her out in the rearview mirror. If he has seen this, however, he is not letting her know anything, and the closer she gets to her apartment building, the more frustrated she becomes.

She crosses her other leg over, lifting her dress even higher until you catch a hint of her soft silk panties. She covers her pussy with three fingers, and then she starts to rub gently on her clit with the longest one. She strains to see whether she is having any effect on the parts of the Ukrainian that matter. Apart from the standard bulge in his jeans that could just be the gentle curve of a soft cock in underwear, she notices nothing.

Leah has about ten minutes before she gets to her apartment, and loses this window of opportunity. She sends her finger underneath the rim of her panties and makes contact with her clit. If this guy doesn't take the hint now, then he is either happily in a relationship, or gay, she consoles herself. She catches his eyes in the mirror, and he almost runs a red light. She reads the question on his face and tries to answer it without words.

Suddenly he is on a side road, headed away from the address she gave him. Much to her relief, he has taken the bait, and soon enough he will be filling her with his sausage until she creams. She cannot think of Tristan right now, or Karl. This is about her, and what she needs, and right now, she needs to be fucked. She keeps her hand where it is to show him that she has not changed her mind.

They pull up beside an old building in downtown LA, and she doesn't have the time to be nervous or scared. He parks his car and takes out a gear-lock. After he has secured the gear lever and the steering wheel, he gets out of the car. He adjusts his dick in his pants so that his erection is not so obvious, and he comes around to her door. He opens it, and steps aside, letting her know that she is required to exit the vehicle.

She gets out and follows him into a warehouse that turns out to be a block of industrial apartments. She has no time to marvel at the architecture or lack thereof. She follows him into what feels like a service elevator, and for a moment she thinks he might take her there and then. Suddenly two hipsters who are either high or just very happy with their lives join them. He presses for the third floor, the hipsters pushing five. The elevator seems to take forever.

When the lift finally stops, he steps out and holds the door open for her. She is soon following him down a very long corridor that has doors on either side, with numbers on them. The doors are so close to each other that she imagines that the spaces behind them must be very small. She doesn't care. She just needs to be somewhere private with this man whose dick is obviously straining to get inside her too.

They finally get to his apartment, and he reaches for the light. She reaches behind him and stops him just before he turns it on. She doesn't want to see what she is about to do. She just wants to feel it, feel him, on her, and in her. He takes the cue perfectly.

She mumbles something about a condom and busies herself with his belt buckle. She struggles a bit, so that he takes out his pack of condoms from his back pocket with one hand, and undoes his belt with the other. He has clearly done this before. Or maybe he frequents the streetwalkers on the LA strip. She doesn't really care right now, just as long as there is the assurance that she will not leave here with herpes.

He isn't wearing any underwear, and Leah cannot hide her excitement. Everything has come into focus now, and she throws her eyes around the small apartment. She sees the usual staples, but no bed. He does have a rather large sleeper couch in the living slash dining slash sleeping area, which is essentially also a large part of the kitchen. She notices the tell-tale signs of bachelorhood but immediately dismisses them. He even has a PlayStation, which also serves as a DVD player since she cannot find one near the TV.

After making her assessment of the space, she deems it clean enough for her to have this random fuck in. She goes down on the tall, handsome stranger, and is relieved to find a perfect twelve-inch boner, neatly circumcised. She takes the head into her mouth and the owner of this perfection winces. He apparently never thought that he would be in this position with a woman like Leah, at least not today, or perhaps not in his lifetime. He holds her head on his dick and starts to thrust excitedly into her mouth.

She can only hope that he is not a premature ejaculator, and she rests the head of his dick deep in her throat. He moans a little more, and she knows that she has him where she wants him.

She knows that he will do whatever she wants him to do to her now, and she can think of a number of things. First on her mind though is that nagging itch deep inside her cunt, where it feels like she has swallowed a large grandfather clock that is ticking loudly away inside her, begging for attention.

When he comes close to blowing his load into her mouth, he pulls his cock from between her lips. She reaches for it, and he manages to move it just out of her reach. He isn't ready for this to be over. He lifts her up off the ground easily and takes her over to the sofa. She helps him help her with her dress, and then she leaves her underwear in his hands. He fumbles for a moment, clearly not a romantic, but soon enough she is naked and lying on the couch, legs spread wide apart.

He looks at her cunt for the longest time, blowing cool air from his mouth over the curls, and then licking it. He does a fucking fantastic job on her clit, and she soon feels like she is close to cumming. Then he goes into her with his tongue, and her orgasm is sent fleeting. He really makes a meal of her pussy, and each time she feels like she might cum, he switches things up so that her climax is once again sent into remission.

Then he lifts her legs onto his shoulder and goes into her asshole. She knows this feeling now. She remembers Philippe. He introduced her to this wonderful technique, but she has been too embarrassed to ask her subsequent lovers to explore this unchartered territory. He digs into her asshole with his tongue so that she sends her own fingers into herself. She cannot help it. It just feels so fucking awesome that she is left wondering what else she can do to this man to thank him. Somehow, she reckons that her pussy will be all the thanks he wants.

He taps on her hand that is in her cunt so that she reluctantly removes her fingers. Immediately they are replaced with his, and the pleasure circuit is complete. She feels like she won't be able to hold herself back from cumming now even if she tried. Fortunately, she has a very high sex drive, so she knows that she will not leave this stranger hanging once she is satisfied the first time.

Leah starts to gasp loudly, two of his thick fingers moving inside her cunt, his tongue licking the inside of her asshole deeply. She cannot hold back anymore. Sharp, shallow breaths follow long, deep ones, as she gets closer and closer. He seems to be determined to draw this first climax from her, and she lets him. She holds his hand in place inside her so that he doesn't even think of breaking the rhythm that has her orgasm more than she can remember for the longest time.

Breathless, she starts to relax every muscle in her body, unable to hold herself up anymore, not needing too, her legs resting comfortably on his shoulders. He keeps his fingers inside her a little longer, his tongue moving in her asshole a little bit more before he finally frees himself from her. He eases her off his shoulders and looks at her lying on the couch. He wants to put his cock in her mouth again, but he is afraid that if he doesn't go for her pussy soon, this offer might not be on the table for much longer.

He wraps up his dick, and she almost giggles at the lumo condom that he is rolling down his shaft. She didn't even know that you get glow-in-the-dark condoms. Clearly, however, you do. It glows a dark blue, and she holds herself back from giggling. He parts her legs again and goes in with his tongue. He just needs to prime her for his cock, which is aching now to get inside her.

She is warm and ready quickly again. She arches her back and raises her pussy into his mouth so that he knows the she is ready for him. She needs him to take her right now, all of her. She has completely forgotten all of her past lovers, and to her own surprise, this stranger seems to have replaced every man that has ever been inside her before. He needs to get inside her now.

He kneels on the couch, between her legs. She raises her knees a little, not too much, and he goes cock first for her cunt. He settles his head inside her just a little and feels for her pussy to give way. It does, willing him inside her. He goes for it, inch by inch, letting her get comfortable with his cock piecemeal. Then he gets all the way inside her and just savors the moment.

His thrust can only be described as comfortable. It is everything that Leah needs it to be and then some. He seems to be able to control his cock now, and he appears to be able to hold himself back from cumming, watching her as she has orgasm after orgasm, watching her writhe under him, and grip him with her nails. He watches her bite on her lip and roll her eyes with pleasure. There is something to be said about being offered pussy that you wouldn't normally be privy to, something that extracts an appreciation from some men. This cab driver is definitely a part of this supportive group. By the time she arrives back home she is satisfied to her core.

10

Leah looks like the cat that got the cream at the boutique the next day. Ray wants to ask her why, but she knows better. She knows that Tristan is out of town, and so she does not really want to get involved. As long as Leah seems to be doing her work very well, she doesn't really care where she gets her world rocked, or by whom.

A bouquet of flowers arrives just after ten, and Ray seems to ignore it so that Leah goes over and takes out the card. *Thanks again, for everything...Ray and Karl!* She hates that the flowers are from both of them, wanting, at least, something, anything, that comes from Karl alone so that she is sure of how he feels about her.

Karl definitely has an addiction to her, physically. How, though, can he just fuck her without feeling anything for her, she asks herself. She is definitely feeling something for him. She has let him know this. She thinks of the wild sex that she had the night before. She didn't feel anything for the man who fucked her, and she didn't even care what his name was. So it is possible, she reasons, to fuck without feeling!

Why then does Karl Von Helsing cause her to come undone like this? Why has she allowed him to get under her skin the way that he has? She wishes that she could just run out of the boutique and be run over by a limousine. Instead, she just smiles, thanks, Ray, and takes the flowers to her desk. After a few minutes, however, she takes them into the main boutique and puts them on the counter, saying something about them being too beautiful to be stuck in the back office.

The many mixed signals that she is reading from Karl are confusing, to say the least. She cannot shake him from her system, no matter how many men she sleeps with in between. Leah just wants him to touch her, to make love to her, to really love her. Instead, he seems to be determined to show her how much he loves his wife. She watches him arrive randomly at the boutique with gifts and flowers. She watches how he kisses her with a passion that is seriously lacking when he kisses her. He does not actually kiss her, really kiss her; he just uses a few kisses to get to her pussy.

She cannot deal with it. However, she wants him anyway that she can have him. If he just wants to fuck her, then he can fuck her. She can only hope that the same shift that is happening inside her each time she is with Karl will take place in him soon. Leah hopes that every time Karl is fucking her brings him closer to this shift.

Karl calls her to his house again. She thinks that he wants her as a style guide again, but Ray has not said anything about it. Leah is not sure if she should tell Ray, and after giving it a bit of thought, she decides not to.

She is really starting to feel the need to create a secret life with Karl, more secret than the fact that he has fucked her in his dressing room, a couple of times, already.

She leaves the boutique just after lunch, lying to Ray that she is not feeling well and that she just wants to go home and lie down. She takes some paperwork with her, to give credibility to her absence from the boutique. Ray is distracted by the work in front of her, so she just kisses the air between them and tells her to feel better. Leah makes her escape and then walks a little down the road before hailing a cab, and taking it straight to the Von Helsing mansion. She goes into the house and finds nobody there. Not even the staff seems to be around, and Leah is a little confused.

She goes out onto the terrace and looks out over the immaculately manicured gardens. She sees a few gardeners working on the hedges, and she suddenly feels safer. This house is enormous, and without movement in it, the walls are very imposing. Then she catches a glimpse of a shadow in the pool house, and she is curious about why Karl would be in the pool house when she expected him to be in the dressing room.

When she walks into the space and finds him naked on the couch, she is glad that she didn't tell Ray that she was coming to her house. Leah puts the files down on the bar counter and her handbag on the floor. She looks at him with a question mark on her face, wondering how he could take such a risk. How could he be so sure that she was not going to rock up here with Ray, and find him naked in the pool house?

She looks at his house again, suddenly nervous about where she is. The pool house has large windows that face the terrace, so that she knows that anybody who came into the house, and looked down at the pool house, would definitely see her in it, alone, with a naked Karl. He doesn't give her an opportunity to speak, however, and he stands in front of her, sending his fingers up her leg almost immediately.

Leah melts into his touch, and closes her eyes again, thinking that she doesn't want to see her being watched, and touched by this married man.

Maybe he knows something that she doesn't, maybe his house staff have the day off, and the gate magically opened itself, maybe Ray won't be home for at least a couple of hours. Still, though, she cannot bring herself to open her eyes. He holds her face in one hand and runs his fingers over her lips. She cannot help but open her mouth and take his fingers into her mouth.

She bites the tip of his finger, and this sends vibrations down to his cock so that it stands rather firmly rather quickly. He sends a finger between her legs and is pleased that she is already moist. He pushes the fabric of her panties into her cunt and then pulls it out. Karl parts her legs a little more and then pulls her panties to the side so that he has direct contact with her pussy now. He loves it. She loves it.

He works his way inside her so that she bites down harder on his finger. It hurts, but it hurts in a good way, and she receives the finger that he is forcing inside her completely now. He fills her up with three fingers and then manages to pull his finger from between her teeth. He uses this now free hand to lift her dress as he works progressively on her pussy. She sweats from deep inside her pussy now, and so Karl can move his fingers around inside her easier than before.

He takes her to the couch, and lays her down on it, her dress above her waist. Karl works her panties down to her ankles and then takes them off her completely. Then he parts her legs wide, and her goes into her pussy with his lips. She holds his head between her legs and squeezes the sides of his face with her thighs. This is the feeling that she loves, and the feeling that she wants to feel forever. There are moments when she thinks that Ray is going to come into the pool house, but then she is brought close to orgasm, and she lets this thought lift from her mind like a veil.

The moment is interrupted briefly when Karl's phone rings, Ray on the other line. She is home, and she has seen his car in the driveway, so she just wants to know where he is. He lies, saying that he was swimming and that he is coming. She must say that she is going to come out because Karl immediately tells her that he is coming inside now, so that won't be necessary.

Leah wants to put on her panties again, and she searches for them quickly. Karl has something else on his mind, however, and he is already rolling a condom down his shaft.

He turns her over and puts her on her knees. He lifts her dress again and picks up her panties. Holding the soft lace in one hand, he sends his cock into her from the back. The squeeze is tight, thanks to the position that she is in, and Karl really enjoys it. He thrusts into her, wildly, and urgently, aiming to cum in under ten minutes. He succeeds too, bringing her to orgasm at the same time that he shoots his load into her, caught thankfully by the condom.

She pulls herself together and heads around the house, hoping to make it to the gate before Ray sees her. Karl takes a quick dip in the pool, easing himself into the water so that Ray cannot hear the splash. When he does go inside, he opens the gate for a moment, and then closes it, hoping that Leah has made her escape. Then he goes to his wife, finding her in the bedroom, waiting for him to welcome her home with his cock. He is more than up to the task.

Leah really tries to dismiss what just happened all the way home. She doesn't get the same Ukrainian cab driver, but she doesn't need him. She pays the cab driver, rushes into her building, struggling a bit with her front door, so flustered is she. Eventually, she is in the safety of her home, undressing, and pouring herself a glass of wine. She takes the whole bottle to the bath and sinks into it.

Karl really is playing a very dangerous game. Leah cannot deny that she likes it a little bit, and it really is a close and dangerous liaison that she cannot resist. She tries to dismiss the thought of him, but he is the only thing that he can think of. How can she win Karl, truly win his heart, and take him from Ray, she wonders? This thought really becomes all-consuming, and she starts to think of Ray as an enemy, in the way of what she has decided that she wants. She really wants Karl Von Helsing.

She resolves to be available for him more, and not to play hard to get. She thinks that the best thing will be for Ray to catch her and Karl in the act. The best way for this to happen is for her to be in their house. She starts to think of how she can make this happen, not even thinking about what this might do to Ray anymore. She has enough money to deal with the loss, and she has the breasts to move on. Leah wants Karl, with every part of her now, and she will take no prisoners in the pursuit of what she wants. There has just got to be a way for her to speed up this exposition.

A week later Ray is working from home. She needs something from the boutique, though, and Leah is quick to agree to bring it over. She has to stop herself from asking if Karl will be there, knowing that this will be weird. She just has to hope that all will go as planned. Leah decides to wait until four o'clock to deliver the items of clothing that Ray wants. She knows that this is the best time for her to run into Karl at his house.

She goes home to change, knowing that Ray will not know this since she was not at the office and she did not see her at all that day. She puts on a white cocktail dress, and perfume, with no underwear. She really hopes that this will be enough for her to seduce

Karl in his home now, not that there has been a problem with him wanting her before.

She gets to the house around seven, and she knows that Ray might not be too happy with her for being so late. She decides to blame it on traffic, inventing a pileup on the highway. Ray squints, so that she knows that she isn't buying it, however, Ray is very pleasant about it. She offers Leah a drink, which she accepts while throwing her eyes around for Karl. She is nervous, thinking that this might not happen tonight, but just then, Karl comes walking down the stairs.

He joins the ladies for a drink, Leah hoping that he notices the absence of underwear. She moves over to the light so that the dress she is wearing is suddenly transparent. Karl eventually catches the fabric and sees right through it. She hopes that Ray doesn't notice this, but she also remembers that the first day she started at the boutique, that Ray had said that she should dress more provocatively.

Leah needs to buy her time; she needs to get Karl alone, somewhere in the house where Ray could walk in on them. She clearly has not thought this through properly because right now Ray is sitting comfortably on her chaise and she doesn't look like she is going to go anywhere. Karl is practically salivating now, but there is very little that he can do about it. He excuses himself, saying that he has a few calls to make in his study.

Leah sees a gap. There is a guest bathroom just beyond the study, and so she says good night to Ray. She lets her know that she is just going to use the bathroom and then leave, so she says her goodnights, pretending to call a cab as she moves out of Ray's eye line. She walks down the hallway and passes the study. The door is slightly open, but she doesn't see Karl inside it. Then he suddenly comes into view, indeed on the phone so that Leah knows that this was not a lie.

She waits on the outside of the door, waiting for him to finish up on the phone. She sends her eyes down the hall, looking to see that Ray will not suddenly make an appearance prematurely, looking for her husband. As soon as he hangs up, she enters the room and pretends to lock the door.

This is her one shot at getting everything that she wants. This doesn't even sound delusional to her anymore, all she knows is what she wants.

Karl is slightly taken aback by this, and he looks at the closed door. Suddenly the tables have turned, and he is no longer in control of the situation. This is obviously very uncomfortable for him, but Leah doesn't care. She knows that she just needs to touch his cock, and it will be game over.

She walks over to him and lifts the skirt of her dress, revealing her pussy, perfectly trimmed, and already beating for him. He tries to resist her, but this resistance is futile. And soon enough she is getting his dick hard with her mouth. There is no time for them to be too creative, however, and so she goes in fast, and she goes in deep, touching herself because she knows that this will excite him. He needs to know how badly she wants him.

Karl is really nervous. However, his body cannot lie, and his erection lets her know that it appreciates the warmth of her mouth on him. His nervousness doesn't seem to affect his ability to sport a massive erection, and Leah knows that she has him. She reaches into her purse and pulls out a condom herself. She manages to get it out of its casing with her fingernails so that she does not have to take Karl out of her mouth.

When she does lift her lips off his cock, she immediately slides the condom over his meat, not giving him a moment to change his mind. He is going to make this quick, and so she hopes that she can keep him inside her long enough for Ray to walk in on them. She pushes Karl's dick down slightly and lifts herself onto her toes. Then she eases him inside her until he is parked firmly in her cunt. He lifts her up and turns so that he no longer faces the door, and Leah's ass is on the large study table.

Karl goes at it with all the anxiety in him. He knows that he cannot disappoint her, not now when she is the one who wants him. He thrusts hard, and she feels him all the way up in her belly. There are few things as passionate as stolen fucking, and Leah starts to feel the beginnings of her orgasm very quickly. She breathes deep and tries not to give away that she is about to cum. Her eyes are fixed on the door, and she starts to hope that Ray will come through it any moment now, she really will not be able to hold out much longer.

Suddenly Ray is calling for Karl, and she feels the thrill of exposure now. It takes over her in waves, and she wraps her legs around his ass to keep him inside her. He wants to pull out. Everything inside him says that he should pull out, now. But she hasn't cum yet, and neither has he. He decides to go for it and try to make it to the end very, very quickly.

Leah makes an adjustment to her ass that throws him off his rhythm; she needs to prolong it just a little more. Karl is not having it, though, and he holds her in place as he rams his cock into her, desperate to cum before his wife walks through that door.

He can explain to her why it was locked. Why it was locked with Leah in the room might be a little more difficult, and this is an explanation that he does not want to have to make. He holds her down firmer, digging his fingers into the sides of her but, and she starts to feel a little uncomfortable. She starts to shake her hips, hoping to pry him loose, but it doesn't help her at all. He is determined to cum, and quickly, very quickly, bring her to an epic orgasm. They are both very close now.

Another person that is close is Ray. The sound of her voice is clear, as though she was in the room with them. Leah looks at the door handle, waiting for it to open at any second. Karl thrusts deeper and deeper, faster and faster. He is cumming now, breathing heavy but careful not to make a sound. She is also cumming, for the third time, and she is unable to hold herself back from letting him know this time.

Then he pulls his cock from her quickly and taking off the condom. He ties it up and wraps it in some tissues from on top of the desk. Leah is disappointed, but she is also gathering herself so that when Ray comes into the room she looks a little less like someone whose husband just ate the shit out of her. She gathers her hair into a bun and wipes some of the sweat from her brow. She determines to get him next time, and she starts to make for the door.

Karl beats her to it, and as he opens the door, Ray is standing on the other side of it. He looks a little flustered but blames it on the phone call. He dismisses the fact that the door was actually not locked, no time to think about this.

She buys it, letting him know that she knows exactly how to get his mind off work. He pulls her close, kissing her while closing the door behind them. Leah hears them playing down the hallway before there is nothing. They must have already gone upstairs. She presses the button that will open the front gate, and then she runs down the driveway just before it shuts again.

She is back in her apartment within the hour. Having a drink, she sits in the dark and thinks about how close she got to Ray finding out about her and Karl. She thinks about the way Karl played with his wife in the hallway, and how ready he always was to make love to her. Her stomach cringes and she feels the pain of loss like somebody just punched her in the gut. Leah tries to drink this feeling away, and soon enough she is opening up a second bottle of wine.

Before too long she is drunk, and looking at her phone. She thinks about calling Karl or texting him. She thinks about it, getting him distracted, just to fuck with him while he fucks Ray. She thinks of calling Ray, and just telling her everything, which will end the lovemaking that she knows is going on at the Von Helsing mansion. She thinks better of it, however, planning to get another chance at Ray walking in on them soon.

She falls asleep on the couch, with her dress over her waist and her hand on her cunt. She tried to bring herself to an orgasm as intense but when it was not happening she just curled up and passed out. She really wants Karl now, more than ever, and if the only way that she can get him is to break up his marriage than that's what she will do. There is no place for emotions anymore or a guilty conscience. She is in LA after all, and people here get divorced every day.

Leah needs to have a hold on Karl that is beyond merely his dick, however, and she decides that she will

do whatever it takes to make that
happen.

11

Leah's hold on Karl seems to be waning, and this is a feeling that she absolutely hates. She never really had hold him to begin with, she admits to herself, but she had made peace with the fact that she never had his heart. She, at least, had a physical hold him, but not anymore apparently. He doesn't even look at her the way he used to when they first met.

This probably has something to with all her talk of love. He must have had his fill of her proclamations, and he must be tired of her whining. She doesn't know what to do. Nothing she does makes him jealous anymore, not Tristan, even though their relationship is getting more and more attention from the public. She really is frustrated. Leah realizes that she really cannot deny that in her mind, there is just one man for her.

Leah needs to up her game if she is going to keep Karl wanting her. She is determined to win him back to her, even if it is just in her bed. She is so consumed with him now that she cannot think past anything else. What can she do to him, for him, with him that she has not already done? What can she let him do to her that he has not already explored?

She goes shopping, online, to try to find other ways to please Karl, and to keep him. The list of tricks is endless; there is really more in the realm of lovemaking than she could ever have imagined. How naïve could she have been, and how could she have been so closed-minded when it comes to sex? She can only hope that Karl will be into some of the new tricks that she is discovering from her little search.

She arranges a meeting with Karl at her apartment. She expects him do deny this, but her persistence pays off eventually. He will arrive after 8, something about having a crisis to attend to at one of his offices, and then having dinner with his wife. She doesn't care too much for the details of how he will escape, concerned only with the fact that he is coming, and that he will see her. She rushes home just after 4 to set things up and to get things ready for a night that she hopes Karl will never forget.

Karl arrives around 10, drunk, and he really looks upset. She just opens the door and steps out of the doorway, giving him space to stagger in. She would have appreciated it if he had the decency to be sober, but she realizes that he probably has had a lot on his mind over the last while, she hopes, at least.

She pours him another drink, against her own better judgment, but she figures what difference can it make? She goes to the bedroom and takes off all her clothes; there will be no time for him to fiddle with trying to get to the places of her that are important to him. Actually, he won't be able to undress her himself, if she has her way.

Leah comes out into the living room and finds Karl seated on the couch. She comes up in front of him and pulls his head into her pussy. He takes a sniff, and she can see that it's game over for him. He cannot hide the fact that she is his Achilles heel. There is a moment's resistance, but only a moment. Then he is reaching for her clit with his tongue.

She pulls away, taking Karl by the hand. He stands up with difficulty, but soon enough he is on his feet. He finishes his drink as she leads him to the bedroom. They get to the room, and she helps Karl onto the bed. She helps him out of his shoes, and then his trousers. She struggles with his shirt, but then Karl is lying on the bed in nothing but his underwear.

She reaches into the side drawer and takes out two sets of handcuffs. Before Karl realizes what is going on, he is cuffed to the bed. He pulls on the furry cuffs, suddenly feeling trapped, hating it. "Relax," she whispers to him and slides his underwear off. One thing she can rely on is the meat between his legs, which is already rock solid so that she wonders if he isn't perhaps popping little blue pills.

Gently, she runs her fingers up and down his legs, stopping just before she reaches his cock, in which his cock is straining now, almost reaching for her touch. She reaches into the side table again, and takes out some oil, vanilla scented. Leah warms it in her hands and then plants her fingers into his thigh. She massages the oil into his legs, and he starts to relax a little more. The alcohol in his head begins to give way to feelings of an erotic nature. He allows it to happen.

Some more oil on her hands warmed up by her fingers; she takes his nut sack in the palm of her hands. She watches as his cock begs for attention, and she runs small circles around his big balls instead. Leah rubs his balls for the longest time, until, eventually, his cock starts to spill a little pre-cum predictably. She knows that she has him literally in the palm of her hands now. And she is enjoying it.

After Karl begs her to pay a little attention to his cock, she does. She runs her fingers lightly up the sides of the shaft so that the tool starts to shake. He wants her to touch it, really touch it. Instead, she just flutters over it with the tips of her fingers. Then she is running her fingernails up and down the tool and a little more pre-cum escapes from the tip.

She straddles his chest and bends down to lick up the warm liquid that escapes his dick. She holds her ass out so that it is close enough for him to smell her cunt. However, he cannot raise his head high enough to reach it. She is very careful about letting him see what he can have without giving it to him, not yet anyway. She just licks the tip of his cock slowly, while holding his big penis upright with both her hands.

His groaning becomes begging, and then loud moaning. She decides to reward him with her lips, placing them up and down his shaft, kissing the surface of his penis hard. Then she takes it into her mouth, and sucks as hard, before she releases it again, and gets back to just licking the head. He trusts upwards, just missing her mouth, the frustration that he is feeling on his cock and in the sounds coming from his mouth.

She bends her ass a little lower, hanging her fruits between her legs just over his lips so that at least he can reach them. He takes her lips between his lips and sucks hard. Then he sends his tongue onto the surface of her cunt and licks up some of the juices he finds there. Just as he gets into it, she lifts her ass and takes her cunt to just out of his reach again. She does reward him, however, sliding her mouth down over his shaft, and settling him deep in her throat.

He cannot take it anymore, hating that he cannot reach the places on her that he wants to. She teases him with her ass, and finally, he gets it. He sends his tongue onto her asshole, and circles it for a bit, and then he is aggressively exploring the inside of it. There are moments where she wants to lift her ass off his mouth, but even she cannot resist the extreme pleasure that this gives her.

Again, she is on his dick with her mouth; over it, using her tongue, and her teeth, then just her lips. She is giving him so many sensations on his cock that he feels like a thousand women are sucking it. She loves the moaning sounds coming from him now, and she keeps doing what makes him moan until all you can hear is one long guttural groan. She really loves this feeling of power.

She rewards him with her pussy now, and he takes it all into his mouth. She practically sits on his face as he eats her out, digging into her with his tongue, sucking hard on her clit. She feels like she might blow at any moment, and so she braces herself. With her hands on his chest and her cunt in his mouth, she lets herself go, and wets his chin and neck with the product of her orgasm.

Leah pulls off his mouth before he can lick up every trace of the warm juices that just flowed from her. She reaches for a condom on the side table and rolls it down his shaft, which is consistently flowing with pre-cum now. She straddles him, facing away from him, with her ass facing his face. He wants to reach out and touch it, but he cannot, the handcuffs doing a good job of keeping him tied to the headboard.

She starts to fuck him, adjusting and re-adjusting herself on his dick until he is all the way inside her. She settles herself over him and grips the side of him with her knees. She squeezes the muscles in her pussy over his cock and starts to move back and forth, slowly. Then she moves a little bit more, lifting her ass slightly so that he can see his dick disappearing inside her. He moans loudly, and she knows that she has hit his spot.

He is also hitting her spot. Karl fills her so much that she needs to adjust again. Once she settles once more over his dick, she starts to move in small circles. Then she moves in bigger circles, giving him further insight into the goings on in her pussy. She doesn't look back, not wanting to see his face, and not wanting to distract him from what she knows he is looking at. He forgets about the handcuffs again and reaches for her hips, but is stopped mid-air.

Leah manages to turn around eventually, Karl still inside her, so that she is now facing him. She takes her hands to her breasts and pulls hard on her nipples. She is really grinding now, and he is moaning almost breathlessly so that she knows that he is close. One thing she is sure of; he will not forget this night. She has firmly re-established her physical hold on him now, and so she brings him steadily to his climax.

She lifts herself off him and plants a kiss firmly on his lips. She explores the inside of his mouth with her tongue, tasting everything that he has drunk that night. The mixture of alcohol is interesting, and she finds herself guessing at the different flavors. By the time she stops kissing him, she has un-cuffed him, leaving him rubbing his wrist. He does not know what to say to her, and so, as usual, he says nothing.

Karl gets up and gets dressed. He has a look on his face that says that even if he did not want to be here, he really enjoyed it. This is just the look that Leah was hoping for. She watches him get dressed and watches as he pours himself another drink. She waits for him to say something to her, but when he does not, she lets it go. He finishes his drink and makes for the door. She watches him disappear down the corridor and into the elevator. Then she takes her satisfaction back to her bedroom.

Karl hates the fact that he was not in

control of the last sexual encounter. He loved the encounter, but the lack of control was foreign to him. He needs to explore other ways for them to satisfy each other if he is to continue this affair, he thinks. He cannot relinquish control of his sexual prowess to a woman, no matter how hot she is, or how good it feels. This is just strange territory for him, territory that he is not yet prepared to explore.

He does see an opportunity, however. There are things, sexual things that he cannot ask his wife to do. Leah, on the other hand, is eager to please, and he suspects that he could probably ask her to do almost anything. Leah is a perfectly suitable partner in the fulfillment of some of his stranger fantasies; he realizes, and so he decides to test the waters.

"Meet me on the beach, in the parking lot!" He gives this instruction and then hangs up; no hello, no conversation, just this instruction to meet him on the beach at nine that night. She thinks he wants to talk, but she knows from experience that he isn't beyond something as juvenile as fucking in a car.

She spots his car at the end of the parking area. She watches as the cab pulls off, and she walks towards the parked car. There are a couple of other cars in the lot, but she determines not to even look inside the cars, keeping her eye on the car that she is approaching. As she comes up on the convertible, Karl gets out, catching her in the side mirror. He watches her as she gets up to the car, and smiles slyly at the short dress she has on.

Karl makes it clear that he does not want to talk when he gets out of the car as she gets to it. As she says hello he shuts her up by putting his long middle finger into her mouth. She closes her lips over the digit, and Karl moves it around in her mouth. She tries to speak again, but Karl just adds more fingers to her mouth, so that she has no choice but to suck on them.

He takes her around to the hood of the car, and lifts her dress, roughly parting her legs. She tries to pull it back down, looking around for eyes that she knows must be there, but she cannot see. Karl pushes her head back and pulls down her panties to her knees. She cannot hide herself now, totally exposed to anyone who happens to look their way.

Then he takes out his cock and pushes her down on it. For the first time that she can remember, it is soft when it goes into her mouth. It doesn't stay soft for long, however, and soon he is sporting a massive erection. Then he pulls her off his cock and holds her legs apart with his knee. Then he works quickly to wrap his dick in the condom that is already in his hand.

She cannot believe this, her cunt not wet at all for the first time since she started fucking Karl. Never have they fucked outside like this, so exposed, in public basically, and she is scared. She never saw herself as much of an exhibitionist, and this is not something that ever crossed her mind. There is no time for her to think about what she does or does not want, however, and soon enough Karl is forcing himself into her dry cunt so that she winces.

He pulls out the part of his cock that he managed to get inside her, and drops some spit from his mouth onto his cock. Then he puts his fingers in his own mouth and transfers some of his own salivae into her vagina. She looks at him with a huge question mark on her face, but again there is no time for her to process what is happening. He gives one swift thrust, and he fills her cunt quickly with his cock. He moves from side to side, trying to distribute the moisture that he added to the equation.

Then he starts to thrust aggressively. He seems determined not to look at her even, holding her face to the side with one hand, the other hand holding her in place on him. He feeds her his dick completely, thrusting against her resistance until she has no choice but to just let him take her. Thankfully, she starts to warm up eventually and release her own moisture, and this makes it easier for her to handle this intrusion. Confusion is written all over her face, and she cannot hide it. He is determined not to see this, however.

Karl cums before she does for the first time. He pulls his dick from her as soon as he does. Then he goes into her raw pussy with his fingers and brings her to her own end. As soon as she cums he removes his fingers from her and turns away. He goes into his car and uses a tissue to dry his hand. She is left adjusting her dress and her mind, not able to make sense of this session at all.

He calls a cab for her and waits until the taxi arrives. Then he winks at her and pulls away before she is even inside the cab. Leah gets home and goes straight to the shower. She never thought that he would make her feel dirty, but that is exactly what he managed to do tonight. He stamped her unequivocally with a label that she had long managed to avoid: *Slut*.

12

There is a sense of relief that Leah starts to feel, however, sensing that she has Karl back in her grip. Love is on the backburner for now, she decides, however, she will take what she can get. There are moments where she feels he might show a little bit of emotion, but then he is leaving her naked, wrapping her fingers around the sheets on her bed, or sorting herself out after an almost public fuck fest, something that she cannot wrap her head around completely just yet.

She wishes that she can take another weekend away to process how she is feeling, but she decides to just accept that she is in absolute love with Karl. She does not know if this is because of the way he treats her; that has her reaching for more than he is prepared to offer, or if maybe, just maybe, she sees in him what Ray saw in him all those years ago when they met.

Ray told her the story of how she and Karl met, and of the journey to where they are now. She listened intently, hoping that she will be given some insights on how to win the billionaire's heart. Ray guards these secrets carefully, however, and so Leah doesn't learn anything helpful about the way to Karl's heart. She decides to leave this at what it is, giving Ray the bragging rights to her man, and her marriage.

What she does notice, however, and something that starts to really bother her is that Karl still hasn't taken her out. She doesn't know what she expects, perhaps that he will show her off in public to his friends, or that, as her relationship with Tristan, she will make it into the gossip pages, holding his hand, or kissing him on the cheeks, or on the lips. This does not seem to be on the cards for them, though, and she starts to accept this begrudgingly.

She scans the social pages more and more, looking for pictures of Ray and Karl. They seem to be everywhere. She feels like his dirty little secret, which is exactly what she is. She starts to wonder if it is her ethnicity, but she knows somehow that it isn't. She could just as easily have been Hispanic or South African, and it would not have made a difference. She accepts her role in this man's life, at least for the present moment.

She does resolve, however, to win him over completely. She has him in her sights, and she starts to imagine herself in Ray's position, as his number one. She sees herself hosting business dinners and frequenting red carpets, with Karl by her side. This leads to a subtle resentment of Ray, and everything that she has. Leah actually gets to a point where she cannot even hold a conversation with her boss anymore.

Ray is oblivious to this change, however, too much going on in her life for her to be too concerned about her PA's mood swings. She has decided that the time has come perhaps to make Leah a junior stylist, but she will have to gain control over her moods first. The last thing she needs is to send her to a client and then receive negative feedback about the interaction. This will impact negatively on her own reputation, a reputation that it took her a very long time to build.

Karl is thinking about Leah, however. He is thinking of how he can use her to fulfill another one of his fantasies. There seems to be a long list of places that he will never even think of asking his wife to fuck at, but Leah on the other hand, is ever eager to please him, and she has not caught on yet that he is just using her to make all his sexual dreams a reality.

He arranges to meet Leah inside the dressing room at a high-end Hermes store in Beverly Hills. It is a little close to her work, a little too close to his wife, but so what. He can easily explain this away, needing to pick up some new ties anyway. Besides, his wife would never suspect that he would be fucking in a dressing room, not when he has access to Ray's hot cunt and perfectly *purchased* breasts at the drop of a hat.

Leah arrives at the store shortly after lunch, and she is surprised by how busy it is. She looks around for Karl, assuming that she will meet him in the ties section, but he isn't there. She walks through the luxurious items on the various stands and imagines herself one day having the purchasing power to walk into a store like this and walk out with what she wants. She cannot help but be star struck, and this has nothing to do with the celebrities all around her.

She gets to the male dressing rooms, and she walks passed them. A door opens, and she recognizes the hand that is calling her into the tiny space. She cannot believe that this is what he wants, but she is desperate to maintain the momentum that she has managed to regain with the relationship. She looks around at the eyes that are not on her, but she is feeling like everybody is looking at her. After a moment's consideration, she disappears into the dressing room, appreciating that it is not the standard curtain covered entrance that she is used to at the places that she shops.

Karl has less than ten minutes,

fifteen at the most to make this work. He lifts her skirt and pulls down her panties quickly. His own cock is already out, firm and wrapped up tightly in the plastic sheath that will stop his seed from spilling into her. He goes down on his haunches and parts her legs with his face, licking her cunt quickly, willing it wet fast. She has no choice but to moisten, both from the sensation, and from memories of using his spit as lubricant. Both these sensations are as different as night and day.

Leah thankfully warms up quickly, and then Karl is standing behind her. He pulls her ass towards him and lifts her onto her toes. He tucks underneath her and drives his cock into her in one swift motion, and she bites down hard on her own teeth. She exhales hard through her nose, knowing that the people in the rooms to the left and right of them will know immediately what is going on if she makes a sound. She closes her eyes, picturing them anywhere but here, needing this distraction if she is going to enjoy it. Leah knows somehow that Karl is not looking at her again, and she again tells herself that this is okay. At least, he still wants her.

Karl thrusts hard and deep, rapid movements of his hips, quick in, quick out. She cannot bring herself to open her eyes, and even tries to imagine that it was another man fucking her. But the scent of Karl Von Helsing is a dead giveaway, and she is brought back to the moment over and over again by the smell of him. There is nowhere for her to move, Karl has her pinned up against the wall with his arm and his cock. She parts her legs a little more, trying to give him more room to move so that this can be over quickly.

To her surprise, she is having an orgasm. She wonders if on some base level something about this primal fucking actually turns her on. She dismisses it, though, knowing that she would much rather be on a bed with him somewhere, anywhere but here. Even if he does not tell her that he loves her. She just wants to get out of the dressing room of this high-end store before somebody finds them. Leah isn't a praying girl, but as the minutes' tick by painfully slowly, she starts to pray that he would just cum already and be done with this. It is all over in nine minutes and thirty seconds.

Leah thinks that maybe she is losing her desire for Karl after all; she does not feel as aroused at the thought of him anymore. Tristan is still in the picture, however, and she tries to form a real connection with him. There is nothing to lose anyway, and she thinks that she may as well give it a shot. However, if Tristan is not fucking her, then she has no thoughts of him, none, not even the inclination to text him. The confusion of it all really starts to take its toll on her, and she starts to realize what people mean when they say that Los Angeles has the habit of swallowing people. Funny, people say the same thing about New York, she thinks.

Fucking Tristan is becoming predictable, however, especially by comparison to her recent escapades with Karl. He doesn't even know it too, it seems, not noticing that the last three times he fucked Leah she was wearing the same lingerie, or that it followed the rather boring suck and fuck regimen that you would see on porn videos. Still, Leah doesn't let him go, part sympathy, part longing for the familiar.

She decides on the night to make it a little interesting. After dinner, they go back to her apartment and manage to make it up the stairs to the front of the building, and into the elevator with Tristan's erection out of sight. She had been sucking his dick in the back of the cab on the way over, much to his surprise, and the taxi driver's amusement. As the elevator starts to move, she presses the emergency button that stops the lift between floors. Tristan looks at Leah, confused, but incredibly aroused.

Leah does a quick job with her own panties, and then she shoves them into his mouth. She goes on her knees and works on his belt, then his zipper, and frees Tristan's cock from its hiding place. She takes it into her mouth and sucks slowly on his meat, making her pussy very wet. She takes one hand to her own pussy, the other holding Tristan's cock in her mouth. Leah works the heat from her fingers into her pussy, enjoying the taste and feeling of Tristan in her mouth. Before she cums, however, she is standing again, and guiding his meat inside her.

He thrusts into her and then stops. Then he pulls out his cock and pushes it back into her slowly. He repeats this a few times, really stirring the pot of love that is between her legs, and frustrating Leah to no end. She pulls him to her when he is inside her again, and lets him know that she is not going to let him go anywhere until he has satisfied her. He takes the hint, fucking her to a beautifully wild orgasm.

Then he brings himself as close to the edge as possible inside her, and at the last possible moment he pulls out of her. She is on his dick with her mouth quickly and soon enough he is spilling semen into her mouth, some of it dripping down the side of her chin. Leah grabs it quickly with her tongue and scoops it back in her mouth. Then she licks her lips and comes up to standing again. She takes her panties from Tristan's mouth and pushes the button that will get the elevator moving again. He is psyched up for a very long night.

13

At least now Leah knows that Tristan is open to alternative fucking locations, but he is definitely no Karl, who seems to be hooked again, albeit to her pussy. Still, Leah is falling more and more in love with him, and she is desperate for his approval. Anything that Karl wants to do, she is prepared to do, and he knows this.

Karl has another idea, deciding to take this up a notch. He arranges another meeting, in the parking lot of the strip mall. Leah doesn't even think that they will go into one of the little cafes in the mall, but since it is still daytime, she doesn't think that he wants to fuck, at least not in the busy parking lot.

She is surprised, as she approaches the car, to see that there is another man in the car. She waits a moment, thinking that she will give him time to finish this meeting. He sees her though, standing close enough to the car to make eye contact with him, and he summons her towards it. She is confused, but nonetheless, she comes right up to the car.

It's not Karl's convertible, but his Mercedes sedan, and she is not sure whether she should get in the back next to the stranger, or get into the front passenger seat next to Karl. She doesn't know, after all, what this man knows about their little affair. Karl signals her with his eyes to get in the back, and after a moment, she jumps into the car next to the strange man.

Leah is shocked to find that the man has a gun, and he is pointing it at her. "Drive," he instructs Karl, keeping his eyes, and gun on Leah. Karl starts the car and pulls away. Leah cannot speak; her mouth is suddenly very dry.

She wonders what the fuck is going on here, and also why Karl seems to be driving in a very particular direction, without any further guidance from this stranger.

They reach a row of warehouses, and go into one of them. The door opens and closes automatically, and Leah knows that this is all staged. Karl obviously doesn't have the ability to be too cloak and dagger, so that he did not think this through properly. Leah is a New Yorker, and she can spot a jig a mile away. She decides to play along, however, just to see what Karl has in mind.

The stranger holds the gun rather convincingly however, and Leah shifts between thinking that this might just be the real thing, and knowing that it isn't. He instructs Karl to sit down on one of the chairs that seem to be too conveniently placed in the space. He pulls the tiny table closer, another convenience, and tells Leah to stand against it. Then he runs the gun over her breasts, and lifts it between her legs, lifting her skirt with the barrel.

Leah wonders what is about to happen, looking at Karl, wondering why he is just sitting there, relaxed. There seems to be no intention to become involved in this, and she wonders just how far this gun-toting stranger is going to go, and how far in fact, Karl will let him go. She pretends to be nervous, pretends to resist when he reaches under her skirt and pulls down her panties. Surely, he will not go all the way. Karl will not allow it.

Then he is unzipping the side of her skirt and pulling it down, rather quickly, the gun pressed up against her stomach. Her panties and skirt gather around her ankles, and she resists the urge to kick them away from her, needing to play along with this charade. The cold barrel of the gun is suddenly pressed up against her pussy, and he is using his free hand to undo her top. He manages to get it off her with one hand, and then manages successfully to remove her bra.

He presses the nose of the gun against her clit, hard, and then drags it up her belly, past her bellybutton, and between her breasts. It is still cold, but she gets used to it quickly. Then the tip of the gun is pressed up against her lips, and she is being told to suck it.

She does, feeling the coolness of the steel on her tongue, and her lips, as he pushes it deeper into her mouth and then pulls it out, in and out, in and out, repeatedly.

He pulls it out of her mouth and runs it over her breasts again, then he places the tip of it on her nipple, one at a time, and then mock-fucks her between her breasts with the full length of the barrel. The stranger puts a finger in his own mouth and wets it considerably, then he parts her legs a bit more and places the finger on the entrance to her cunt. He wouldn't dare she thinks, but soon enough he is going into her with the long, wet finger. She cannot believe it, not allowing herself to think that he will enter her until just now.

She throws her eyes at Karl, who has a smirk on his face, like he is really enjoying this. He is, obviously, and she decides to see how much he will enjoy it if she enjoys it. Leah starts to moan loudly and she holds on to the side of the table. She thinks of taking her breasts into her own hands, but thinks that this will be too much so she just keeps them at her side, holding herself up against the table, moaning with each movement of the finger lodged deep in her cunt now.

The stranger kisses the side of Leah's face, and the lick her up her cheek several times, looking to Karl, obviously for direction. Leah does not see Karl not, and so she doesn't know that he is urging the man to go all the way, but with his finger already inside her, and his tongue on her face, she is sure that this is not where it will end. She wants to reach for his cock too now, but she restrains herself, knowing that this will certainly be too much. She just keeps on moaning as the finger in her gets more aggressive.

She cannot help the warmth developing in her pussy now, and she starts to release some warm, sticky liquid from her depths, and the finger in her moves around easier. Then the stranger's mouth is on hers, the barrel of the gun still moving consistently between her breasts, and another finger added to her cunt. Then these two fingers are moving around inside her cunt and she is really enjoying it, but moaning loudly now even with the man's lips on her.

Then he is kissing her neck, aggressively, and the stubble on his face tickles her, but not in a way to make her laugh. It is very erotic, and there are moments again that she just wants to reach for him and touch his dick. There are moments when she just wants his dick inside her, any dick actually, but she knows that she must just be patient and wait it out; it will not be long before one of them at least is fucking her.

The barrel of the gun moving between her breasts now is moving with the same rhythm and intensity as the two fingers inside her pussy, his mouth locked on hers now so that she is breathing into his mouth, unable to move away from his mouth even when it becomes difficult for her to breathe often. She decides to concentrate on breathing through her nose now, because there is no other way to get the air into her lungs that she needs.

There is no way for her to hold herself back from cumming now, and she can only hope that he will not remove his fingers from her prematurely. He does not, pushing the two fingers deeper inside her, harder and harder, until she is having a spontaneous eruption. He adds another finger into her dripping pussy now, and moves the three fingers around inside her so that she feels like three cocks are fucking her. His fingers are thick, and she finds herself making a quick comparison with Karl's hand.

He pulls more moisture from her, running his fingers wildly across all the walls of her pussy, and hitting the back of it with his longest finger. He is really into it now, and Leah has to hold on tighter to the table. Fortunately, the table doesn't seem to want to go anywhere, because if it moved just an inch, she would be hitting the cement. The gun is no longer riding her tits. In fact, it is on the floor near the stranger, who is now on his knees, sniffing her pussy, longing to take a lick.

Then he looks at Karl, who nods again. He smiles, and unzips his pants while he puts his tongue on Leah's clit. He licks it aggressively, his tongue dry and rough. He must smoke a hell of a lot, Leah thinks. Then he is trying to join his tongue with his fingers inside her fanny, not getting too far. Reluctantly he removes all his fingers and places his hands on her thighs. He holds her firmly in place, and drives his tongue into her cunt with real gusto.

He eats out her pussy like a ravenous dog. Reaching for his cock, as soon as he has gained momentum, he pulls it out through the zipper. Leah cannot see it yet, but she hopes that it is at least as big as Karl's. Then she can really have fun with it, knowing that the control freak in Karl will not be able to stand a man with a cock similar, or hopefully bigger than his fucking her.

His tongue works the inside of her pussy until again she is creaming. Then he stands up and repositions Leah so that Karl has a front row seat to the penetration. She takes some more of the cream from her pussy and rubs it on his cock, which is at least two inches bigger than Karl's, although you would never have guessed it, the stranger much shorter than the German. He pulls on his cock hard, making sure that he has every inch right down to the base outside of his pants. Only his balls remain covered by the denim.

He places his cock between Leah's legs and watches her face as he starts to insert the meat into her wet and waiting cunt. He goes in slow and deliberate, making sure that Karl really has the best view in the house. Karl cannot help but touch his own cock now, and this Leah does see. At last, he seems to be responding to the scene playing out in front of him. He is really running his fingers along his lengthy shaft now, but Leah tries not to give this too much attention. She has enough to keep her mind, and body occupied, and she returns her focus to the anaconda making its way inside her.

She knows that Karl will not masturbate, but he may as well be with the aggressive way that he is now rubbing his dick. He goes so far as to undo his belt and unbutton his pants, putting his hand inside it, to touch his meat directly. He strokes his dick now, slowly, but not masturbating still. He will want to be inside her soon enough and he seems to have the patience of a saint.

The dick inside her fills her up completely, and she forgets even about

Karl for the moment. He moves back slightly, and Karl watches as the barge pole penetrates Leah with a verve and excitement that sees him pull harder on his dick. There really is so much pleasure to be derived from watching porn live like this, especially when Karl knows that he is the mastermind behind it. He watches her face, seeing that she is really enjoying it, hating it but also not.

He wants to get up and move the man with the huge cock aside, move him outside of this woman who he had long convinced himself that he was the only man for, the only one who knew how to touch her. He does not though, remembering that he promised this man that he would get to fuck her until he blows. Karl relaxes into his seat therefore, and pulls steadily on his dick. It isn't as satisfying for him though as he thought it would be.

The stranger really drives all the way inside Leah now, and she gasps, trying to catch her breath and hold on to the table at the same time. She throws her fingers around his neck, holding herself up now as he thrusts inside her incessantly. He holds her by her hips now, pushing her away from him slightly so that the view is not obstructed. What he wants to do is pull her fully onto his cock, but he too remembers the deal that he made with Karl. Still, he manages to thrust completely into her so that she is again moaning very loudly.

He feels the beginnings of a climax start to stir inside him, and he slows down. He doesn't want to cum too quickly, really enjoying this wet pussy that is so eager to swallow every inch of him into itself. He runs his cock up one side of her pussy, then the other side, and then he hits the back of it with his massive head until Leah is practically screaming. She cannot help it. It feels fucking fantastic, and she has all but forgotten that Karl is right there watching them. Maybe he thinks it is for his benefit that she is putting on this performance. But Leah isn't acting, really enjoying the shit out of this mammoth cock.

Then Karl stands up and whips out his own cock. Leah looks at him, the satisfaction hanging in her eyes so obvious that he doesn't want to look at her. He comes up close to them, and the stranger thinks for a moment that he is going to move him. He doesn't. Instead he parts Leah's ass and rubs his dick between the cheeks, needing the warmth, longing himself to be inside her. She doesn't care what he does now. She is too focused on the guy who is absolutely obliterating her pussy. She makes a mental note to get the morning after pill when it seems like he will not be able to stop himself, or pull out of her hot pussy in time.

With Karl no longer looking at the fucking that they are doing, the stranger pulls Leah towards him a bit more and settles her completely and he lowers himself slightly to give his thrust some traction. He digs into her from his new position and Karl gives him a moment to settle into this movement. Then he pulls her asshole towards his meat again and continues to rub his dick between her cheeks. He knows that he won't resist the urge from entering her for too long, and he is willing to settle for her ass for the moment, until his friend is done with her pussy.

Karl does not wet his cock. There is enough sweat dripping from Leah's ass to allow him to ease his cock into her ass easily. He is surprised by how quickly she takes him, and his mind goes to all the other guys who have probably had the pleasure of fucking this perfect ass. He drives his dick into her asshole completely to secure his place in her life. She squeezes her butt-muscles around his cock and he knows that he has possibly gone too deep. He pushes a little deeper, needing to make his presence felt. Again she squeezes her ass around his cock, and again he pushes in a little deeper.

Leah decides to let him take her completely, and do what he thinks he needs to do. There is nothing that she can do to stop him now, anyway; so she returns her focus to her pussy. The stranger is working aggressively on her cunt again so that she doesn't have to think too hard about this penetration. She feels like she is about to cream again, and so she settles into the dick inside her more completely, taking some of her ass off Karl's cock. Sandwiched between these two dicks she starts to lose herself in the moment, and quickly, very quickly, she is creaming.

The stranger seems like he is not any closer to cumming then he was when he began fucking her now though, and she is really getting tired. There is no time for her to be tired now though, with both men really digging into her now, both of them really making every effort to draw another orgasm from her. They are not even aware that she has cum already, for the fourth or fifth time, and they just continue drilling her two holes. Then the stranger suddenly picks up the pace, and he closes his eyes. Leah knows what this means, and she thinks that he deserves the pleasure of cumming inside her. She cannot bring herself to evict him from her pussy now, and she is thankful for the advances in medicine that will make it possible for her to have him cream inside her without leaving her with a nasty surprise.

At the last possible moment though, the man pulls his massive cock from her and takes it into his own hands. She looks at his fingers moving rapidly up and down his shaft and she wonders if she will get there in time. She will try though, and she bends her back and brings her head over his throbbing cock, taking it into her mouth very quickly. He appreciates this, and starts to thrust into her mouth, not minding the teeth at all. Soon enough he is coating the inside of her mouth with his semen, and he is the one screaming now.

Karl appreciates the bend too, since this feeds him more of Leah's ass. He too is thrusting aggressively into her now, at a consistent pace, needing to cum. He fucks the shit out of her literally, and when he too is cumming, there is no need for him to bring himself out of her. He thrusts persistently until his dick is completely milked by her asshole. There is a deep sense of satisfaction on his face, and he doesn't even try to take his dick out of her asshole. Then he pulls her up so that her back is against his chest, his dick still hard, and still firmly lodged inside her asshole. There is no rush for them to gather themselves or for them to move out of the warehouse just yet, Karl owning it.

Karl takes Leah's breasts into his hands and kisses her on the mouth while guiding the stranger down with his eyes back onto her pussy. He wastes no time and goes down on her pussy with his mouth. He sucks the juices out of her cunt and sends his tongue into her. Very quickly he settles into her completely, enjoying all the flavor that he finds between her thighs. He pulls away from her pussy a moment, and licks the sweat from her thighs before returning to her cunt and absolutely devouring it.

With his mouth still on her lips, Karl watches closely as his friend prepares her pussy for one more round. He pulls his dick from her asshole slowly, still kissing her, and then he makes his way to the front of her. He taps his friend on his shoulder, and reluctantly the man relinquishes control of her pussy and stands up, giving Karl the space he needs to put himself inside her. He takes a moment to appreciate the beauty of her cunt, and then he is moving his dick inside it. He doesn't stop until he is all the way inside her, and if he could get his balls into her pussy too, that is exactly where they would be.

He remembers how his buddy fucked her slow and steady, and he decides that he is going to go for it with all the power his dick can muster. He needs to be different; he needs to be memorable. He thrust hard into every part of her pussy, rubbing his dick hard against every wall, digging deep into every corner of her cunt. It is wet, and it is fiery hot, and he loves it. He feeds himself into her almost angrily, and he holds her firmly in place so that there is no chance of her escaping this invasion.

She realizes that this is all a game to Karl, and she actually doesn't care anymore. He is thrusting into her violently now, and she wishes that the stranger could take over on her ass so that she can think of something else. She doesn't want to enjoy Karl, but against her own better judgment, she has to admit to herself that she is. She probably will for the longest time too, she thinks. Fortunately, she feels a finger inside her asshole, and she knows that he wants inside her. There is a moment where she thinks she might even pray just to thank god for this attention.

He works up to three fingers in her asshole, and she appreciates the stretch. She is quickly forgetting about Karl moving in and out inside her pussy, knowing that the man in her asshole is preparing her for his dick. She wishes that he would get his cock inside her already, but she knows that he feels the need to stretch her a little more. Soon enough, though, he is easing his massive head inside her, and she loves it. He is obviously too big for her, but she is determined to take all of him inside her, or at least as much of him as will fit inside her tight asshole.

He thrusts into her easily, and the sweat from her crack falls into her hole, onto his cock, making this easier. Karl is close now, and she doesn't even feel the need to think about what he will do with his seed, or where he will deposit it. All her energies are focused on the rod in her asshole, also close to cumming from the sounds escaping his mouth, but not fucking her with any more aggression than when he started. Karl shoots his load deep inside her pussy, and she makes a note to remember to visit the pharmacy in the morning. She returns her focus quickly to her ass, and she bends far forward and lets the stranger ride himself to the best end.

There is a moment when both men stop moving around inside her. Then the guy in her ass is thrusting again, and his dick is getting hard again. Karl looks like he doesn't need this competition, and he pulls his dick from her pussy. He pulls her mouth over his meat, and he too is soon sporting another erection. He watches her mouth moving over his cock, and he cannot hide the fact that he loves it. He holds her hair up and out of the way so that he can watch this exercise.

She braces herself on his thighs and keeps on working on his dick while the stranger in her ass really goes to work on her ass again. The semen that is filling her ass makes it easier for him to move his mammoth tool around in her ass and he appreciates this. He holds her by the hips and pulls her onto his cock now, steadily, without disturbing the oral action being dealt out on Karl. There seems to be no hurry again, but Leah is getting really tired, her knees feeling like they are going to give in at any moment.

Karl lifts her off his mouth and finds

her pussy again with his dick. Again he has no condom on, but he doesn't seem to care. There are ways to sort this problem out in the morning, and he is aware of them. The stranger comes closer to her now, still holding her hips, still pulling her towards his cock, getting himself closer and closer to another climax. He does a great job on her ass, and soon enough he is spilling seed into her tight asshole again. Then he pulls out and walks away, sorting himself out as he goes.

Karl lifts her off her feet and places her ass on the table. He really digs into her now and gives it everything that he has in him. There are moments when he thinks for the first time that he might lose his erection, but he just has to look down at his dick moving in and out of this black beauty, and he is rock solid again. He thrusts harder, deeper. Then he thrusts slowly, making her cum with a few slow strokes before he brings himself closer to the edge.

Then he pulls his dick out of her pussy suddenly, and he turns her over. He bends her over on the table and holds on to her breasts again. He allows her the time she needs to adjust herself on the table and to find her feet, and then he is driving into her with his dick again. He goes passed her asshole and into her pussy again, knowing that this change in position will give her the momentum she needs to handle the rest of the experience. She is really tired, and sweat is running down her back now. The new position also allows him to squeeze her thighs together and give his lengthy cock more contact with her flesh.

The stranger is sitting now, watching them, having no problem masturbating as he does. He really enjoys this view, and he pulls hard on his cock, which is exposed again and throbbing. He runs his fingers up and down his shaft almost as aggressively as he fucked her in her pussy and her ass and he is soon enough gaining the momentum that he needs to take himself to the edge. He wishes though that Karl had the decency to turn them so that he was able to watch them fucking without having to look at Karl's ass.

Karl is really digging into her pussy now, getting some serious traction so that her cunt is practically pulling on the surface of his shaft. He lets go of her breasts and almost leans back so that he can watch his dick disappearing into her and moving around inside her. He holds on to the table again, when he feels like his own legs might give in, and then he drives into her hard. The stranger watches as his balls move around outside her pussy, knowing that his friend has gone all the way into her. There is no turning back now, nowhere for her to run, and nowhere for him to go but deep inside her pussy, taking them both over the edge. She falls onto the table on her forearms, needing to hold herself up but knowing that this will not last very long.

After the longest time, Karl pulls his dick from her, and he sorts himself out. He goes to where his friend is sitting and takes a seat next to him. They both watch as Leah gathers herself, completely exhausted, and looking like she needs a shower. They drive her to her apartment, and Karl makes sure that she is okay when they get there, leaving her on the outside of the building, though, not going in. She goes upstairs and heads straight to bed. She will shower later, and rid herself of all the semen inside her. For now, though, she needs to sleep, and she needs to process everything that has happened to her with Karl and his friend.

She tries to hide her face from the thoughts that are creeping up on her. But she doesn't have to hide too long because soon enough she is fast asleep and dreaming of everything but.

14

Leah walks into the boutique the next morning and is surprised to see Karl eating a bagel in the front of the store. His wife is busy with paperwork in the back, and so she cannot see them. She greets him, and the cold reception she receives from him surprises her even more. Is it because of the way she enjoyed the stranger's dick the day before, she wonders. He set it up, though, so this is very strange indeed. She decides to ignore the lack of attention that she is getting from him, and put it off to a bruised ego.

Even in the days that follow, though, Karl is exceptionally cold towards her, so that it actually starts to bother her. What reaction did he expect from her? Did he expect her not to enjoy the fucking? Did he expect her to be scared, and to carry this fear throughout the engagement? How could he be so selfish? She accepts that he is just a self-centered bastard, and she tries her best to ignore this situation.

She yearns for his attention, however, and really wants him more and more with each day that passes. There are days when she tries to get him alone, and there are days when she tries to blow it off, but then there are days when she genuinely does not care. The days that she does not give a damn are rare, though, and she cannot resist the urge of trying to get him alone, just so that she can feel his hands on her. That is why when he eventually texts her, demanding that they meet, she is so excited that she goes home to shower and change, a few times until she is sure that she looks as irresistible as she suddenly feels again.

"We cannot see each other anymore!" he says, when she walks into the hotel

room that she thought would be their love nest for the afternoon.

"I don't understand!" she replies, not sure if she is hearing him correctly.

"Of course you do...it has been a lot of fun, and it has been interesting...but we just cannot do this anymore!" he says, determined it seems to make his point.

She takes a while to process this, walking to the window of the room and opening the curtains, then the window. The breeze caresses her face, but it does not blow away the words that she has just heard. They ring inside her head like an alarm, and she cannot shake the buzz from the space between her ears. There is nothing that she can do to change his mind, apparently, and she is not in the mood suddenly to even try. There are times that she could not imagine not fighting for his attention, but this is not one of those times.

She decides that it is over and that she should accept it. She looks at him looking at her, waiting for her to say something, probably expecting her to offer up more of a protest, more resistance to this decision that he has taken alone, but she has nothing for him. There is no fight in her, the feeling of being punched in the gut-filling her over and over again in waves, and leaving her feeling quite winded. She sits on the bed; then she is standing again. She paces the room, trying very hard not to look anxious or distraught. She cannot even look at Karl anymore, thinking of everything that she has been through during the last while in an attempt to please him and keep him happy.

"Can I ask you one thing then, and then you will be free to go...," she asks him, not sure if he is going to agree with what she has on her mind, but needing to ask him anyway.

"Ask...," he says, looking away from her again.

"Can you make love to me...really make love to me...just so that the last memory I have of you is not as part of a threesome?" She is looking at him now, needing to see what he thinks because suddenly he is the one who is quiet.

He walks to the window now, the curtain and window still open, so that he too is standing directly in the breeze. He looks around the room, needing a drink suddenly. Karl cannot find the fridge, though, and he starts to get edgy. She watches him closely now, needing him to respond to her quickly before she leaves this room and walks out of his life forever. Then he suddenly starts to unbutton his shirt, and she takes this to mean that he will, at least, give her this one thing. She takes off her panties, knowing that he will not want to struggle with her underwear and that he will just want to get out of here.

Leah watches as Karl takes off his shirt and puts it on the chair. Then she watches as he removes his trousers while working on her dress, then her bra. She sits naked on the bed and watches as Karl removes his underwear. She never thought that this is how it would end, but she feels it in her heart, and in the pit of her stomach that it is really over. She makes up her mind to really enjoy this, and not to do anything unique or fancy, just to allow Karl to fuck her the way that he wants to. She can only hope that he will make love to her with a little more attention to detail, and make this night a night to remember.

Karl realizes that she deserves this, at least, given everything that she has put up with over the last while. There is no denying that he finds her attractive sexually, his erection evidence of this. He goes over to the bed and takes her face in his hands, and he pulls her up off the bed so that she is standing in front of him now. She is much shorter than he is, and he has to really bend to kiss her. He cannot remember the last time his really kissed her, and he pulls her tongue into his mouth before placing his in her mouth. They kiss for the longest time, and when he pulls his mouth away from hers, she knows that this was the last time that she will feel his lips on her like this.

He touches her between her legs tenderly, and she starts to shiver, never thinking that he was capable of this tenderness. She settles into the feeling, needing him to take her completely one last time, and make every second count. She parts her legs a little more, giving him more access, more space, and he runs the tips of every one of his fingers over her clit. She is warm and wet very quickly, but she does not tell him this. She does not need too because he is soon feeling around the inside of her cunt with the tip of his index finger.

Then he is kissing her neck, and she drops her head back to give him the space that he needs to work. He kisses her gently up and down her neck, and she closes her eyes and takes a deep breath. There is something definitely different about the way he touches her tonight, and she is really pleased that he agreed to take on one more ride along the scenic route. Then he is suddenly on her breasts with his lips, and she feels the warmth from his mouth transmit into her.

He works them onto the bed, and when he has her on his back, he goes between her legs. He kisses her gently on the inside of her thighs, and then on her clit. Then she is holding his head in place, and he is licking the inside of her pussy with his tongue, deep, and making her squirm. There is no thought of the conversation that got them to this point anymore, just this moment. It is beautiful, and she has the feeling that she is close to cumming. She does, and he laps up every drop of moisture that comes out of her. He practically drinks up the liquid, really going for it, enjoying this last taste that he is going to have of the fruits of this woman's love vine.

Then he comes up to her mouth again, and again he is kissing her. She is grateful for this second kiss, and she makes it really long and deep. She allows her mind to go to that place where he loves her back the way she loves him, and this sends feelings to her legs that she last felt when she was in high school. Her first time was special, and it was with someone that she thought would love her forever. That was a long time ago, though, and she resolves to be completely present in this moment.

Then he is on her neck again, not kissing her, but pulling in deep and hard, sucking the blood towards the surface of her skin so that she knows that it will leave a mark. She doesn't mind. Nothing matters now, and she is going to give him everything that he wants tonight. She is going to give herself up to him, heart and soul, and body of course, and not think about the fact that this is the last time that he is going to touch her like this again. She runs her fingers up and down his back, needing him to know just how thankful she is for every single experience that she has enjoyed at his hands.

She cannot deny that even the times when he was just fucking her were incredible. All that power thrust into her, making her feel like he was transferring himself to her, really will make for great memories. There is not a single bad memory that she will have of this man. She just has to accept that his wife won in the end, as it should be, and she dismisses thoughts of Ray that creep up on her. There is no place for a third person in this room now, not now, not ever.

Karl finds her nipples with the inside of his mouth again, and again she shudders. She really wants him inside her now, and she cannot even hide this from him. She tells him to make love to her, but he responds *not yet*. Could it be that he also does not want this to end? Why then would he end this affair? What could she have done to make him not want to fuck her anymore? Could it be that he has had an epiphany and that he just realizes that he really loves his wife?

She tries hard not to think of this. The thoughts nag at her, however, so that she needs something to distract her from her own head. She lifts him off her breasts and slides down under him until she can take his cock into her mouth. He thrusts gently into her mouth from the top, and she needs to concentrate on this cock that is moving around inside her mouth now. She appreciates this distraction and gives her all to sucking Karl's massive dick.

She sucks his meat as he gently fucks her mouth and she is surprised when he is suddenly cumming in her mouth. She did not expect it, and almost chokes on his semen. She gathers herself sufficiently, though and manages to swallow every drop. She sucks on his meat for a while longer and then eases him out of her mouth. Leah hopes that this is not the end of it, and she just stays put underneath him. Karl is the one working his way down on her now, settling comfortably between her legs, and then turning over so that she is sitting on his face. He eats her out steadily, and she loves every moment of this.

She grinds her pussy into his mouth, and Karl just continues to have fun with it. He seems to be enjoying himself too, and whatever tension there was in the room earlier has all but dissipated. Right now there are just two human beings who want nothing else but to fuck the shit out of each other. Both parties are incredibly patient now too; it seems, having had their first orgasm already so that the edge is taken of them slightly. They can now just enjoy each other's bodies thoroughly.

He brings her to another incredible orgasm, and she falls onto the bed. Karl quickly assumes his position on top of her again, and he is again on her mouth. All this kissing is enough for her to delude herself into thinking that the conversation that she now thinks they had earlier did not in fact happen. Leah goes for it again, kissing him deeply and passionately. She wishes that they had ordered a bottle of champagne into the room, but it is too late to think of this now. She does not want to say or do anything that will end this too soon.

Karl's dick is aching to get inside her now. It is throbbing, and the tell-tale vein on the side of it seems ready to burst. She places her hand on his meat, and guides him into her depths, enjoying it like it was the first time. Everything, in fact, feels new and fresh and different. She wishes that this night could last forever, but with Karl now thrusting his hot rod into her, she knows that it will probably come to an end very soon. She works with him, grinding in direct opposition to his thrusts, and the moment seems to be soaked in perfection.

He still doesn't appear to be in any rush to go anywhere, and he definitely is in no hurry to cum. As long as he has his meat where it wants to be, he is incredibly happy. He looks at her face, watches her with her eyes closed, really enjoying this, enjoying him, and he smiles. If they had perhaps met in another time, another life, perhaps then he might have been able to offer her something more than just sporadic fucking. This life was not meant for the two of them, however, and he has an inkling of regret.

She opens her eyes and catches his

gaze. She holds it for the longest time, thinking that she can read his mind. If she could read his mind, she would hope that he would be apologizing for the terrible inconvenience that he was in her life, making her believe in something that she really could not have. There is something to be said for timing, and unlike Karl's perfectly timed thrusts, this time, does not seem to belong to them in any way, shape, or form. She settles under him as he drives his dick deeper and deeper into her pussy, slow, gentle strokes that the animal that fucked her just a few days before. This is how she wants to remember him, at this moment, doing this to her. This is how she will remember Karl Von Helsing.

15

They make love; really make love, and it is everything that Leah ever imagined that making love to this man would feel like. She takes a moment to take it all in, and then allows Karl to extract his penis from inside her. She thinks that she knows what will happen next, that he will get dressed in silence and then leave. Instead, he jumps off the bed and goes to the bathroom. After a long pee, he comes back into the room and takes the phone off the hook, holding it to his ear while running his fingers up and down her legs.

He orders some food for them, and two bottles of champagne. Leah relaxes into the evening now, realizing that Karl does not intend to leave the room anytime soon. She wants to reach out and hold him, but she holds back, knowing that this night has got to be about what he wants and that she cannot give him the inclination that she is reading more into the situation than what there is. The food and drink arrive, and they eat, chatting easily about everything but the elephant in the room.

She is okay with it too, thinking that this is a great last date, and she could not have scripted it better herself even if she tried. Karl pours them champagne, and they take it to bed with them. They play and laugh, and she is again going to that place in her head where he belongs to her. She knows better, though, and so she does not say anything. The first bottle goes down quickly, and the second one is opened. They drink, Leah hoping that she does not lose her inhibitions and starts again with her childish proclamations of love.

There is no time for any proclamations. However, Karl is making love to her again. It is more intense this time, familiar territory for her and Karl, and she enjoys it. Karl cannot resist fucking her a few more times too, sealing this relationship if you could call it that, with a mind-blowing orgasm. Leah falls asleep in his arms, and she loves the smell of him. So comfortable is she in fact, that even when they wake up together, she feels like she is dreaming. He fucks her with his morning glory, turning it into the most glorious morning, and then after telling her to order what she wants for breakfast, he kisses her on the lips, showers, dresses, and leaves.

That is the end of Karl Von Helsing; she tells herself, but it least he sent her off into the world with an absolute bang.

She orders breakfast and reads the note that Karl left for her. It is short and sweet, telling her that it has really been an experience knowing her, but he needs her to remove herself from his life now. By this, she takes him to mean that he wants her to leave her job and possibly get out of LA. Again she has old feelings of being gutted, but she understands what he means and where he is coming from.

She works for Ray for another two months, however, needing to work her notice period in with the boutique owner to ensure that she gives her a great reference. Karl makes no appearances at the boutique in these two months, and Ray does not call on Leah to style her man anymore. Could she somehow have found out about the affair, Leah wonders? But how could she know, and still seem so torn that she wants to leave her employ?

On the last day that Leah is in the boutique, it is a bittersweet moment. She has a glass of champagne with the woman who gave her a first real break in LA, and then she goes back to her apartment. She sits on the couch and thinks about the last year, and everything that has happened. She remembers all the men that fucked her, and she thinks especially of the Frenchman. Tristan is on her mind too, but that is long over. Leah has a couple of critical decisions to make, and she thinks hard about the way forward.

Ray gave her a large check when she left, and Karl too presented her with a gift, largely unexpected, but accepted at his insistence. So she has a good deal of money to get her set up somewhere else. She thinks San Francisco. She starts to plan her move and gives notice to her landlord. It is close enough to LA for her to still pursue her dreams of being a stylist, she tells herself.

One thing has bothered Leah though, since the last time she fucked Karl. He did not wear a condom at any time, and he fucked her often. She has had her period, so the thought of her being pregnant never even crossed her mind. She has been sick, however, but she put this down to nerves at the changes in her life. She runs her fingers over her belly and wonders, though. Could she be pregnant? And if so, what does this mean for her and Karl? Is this even an option?

She goes out and buys a home pregnancy test. She is too scared to use it, though, and she decides to leave it in her medicine cabinet in her bathroom. She cannot face this possibility, not yet anyway, and she is too late to even think of an abortion if she fell pregnant the last time she was with Karl. *Fuck, fuck, fuck*, she thinks.

Leah decides to go out, just to get

her mind off the man who might have left her with a little more than just a goodbye fuck. She cannot drink, so she doesn't, but she decides to just sit at the bar in a nearby club and have virgin mojitos. She will do the test tomorrow; she convinces herself. Tonight, though, she will just try to forget everything that she has done here, all the damage that she has caused.

A group of men comes into the club, obviously too old to be in here, but obviously dripping with money. She thinks that their perfect little wives must be waiting for them at home, living pampered lives that made the occasional boy's night out acceptable. This was Los Angeles though, she tells herself, and here, more so than anywhere else in the country, there seemed to be no age restriction on partying.

When one of the men catches her eye, she looks away. She is not up to this, not tonight. She has a lot on her mind, and the last thing she needs is to wake up in a stranger's hotel room, throwing up. Then he is walking towards her, and she cannot escape him. He puts a hand over her hand and runs his thick, stubby fingers up and down her arm.

"How much?" he asks her, and she realizes that he probably thinks that she is a whore. Can a black woman not come out on her own without the whole fucking world jumping to fucking conclusions, she thinks? At that moment she remembered Karl, thinking that for all intents and purposes, she had been his whore for a long time, and received a lump sum once her services were no longer required. Before she can stop herself, she is walking out of the club with the short, stocky billionaire and leading him to her apartment, which is just a few blocks from the club.

She has not mentioned a fee, so she has not solidified her status as a prostitute. But the guy looks like he hasn't had a decent fuck in a while, and she could use a little *grateful* attention on her pussy before the morning comes and she has to face the reality of her life. They make it to her apartment in silence, and as soon as they enter the space, he is suddenly very active. He is holding her close to him, wanting to kiss her on her mouth, Leah giving him her cheek. She remembered reading somewhere that whores don't kiss on the mouth.

She gets him out of his clothes, and then she gets out of her clothes quickly before she changes her mind and has the poor man leaving in an awkward huff. She goes for his underwear, and finds a perfectly adequate erection between his thick thighs. He will not hit her spot, she knows, but at least, she will have an orgasm, and she will have done her bit for charity. She goes down to meet the thick dick with her mouth, and she parts her lips, taking it into her mouth inch by inch. She tells herself that she can at any moment tell him to leave, so she just decides to enjoy this.

Leah really does love sucking dick, any dick, and this shows in the way she handles the meat in her mouth. The john is mumbling something, but she doesn't care very much about how good she is making him feel. This is all about her, and what she needs to do to get her mind off her little problem. She is licking the head of the thick cock, and the man is going crazy. He has obviously never had someone go down on him with so much attention to detail.

She could not help but think that he would have a bigger penis if he lost a little bit of weight. This is no time for her to hand out any advice on the man's lifestyle, however, so she decides just to focus on the matter of sucking on his dick. He doesn't give any sign that he is about to cum anytime soon, and soon enough, her jaw takes strain. She has had longer dicks in her mouth, but few as thick. No matter how much she is enjoying sucking on this fatness, she needs a break.

Leah wonders if she should offer him a drink. Before she can, though, he is on his knees and eating her pussy out carelessly. It is not uncomfortable, or not enjoyable, but the woman at home, the woman in this man's life, must not like being gone down on so that he has not had a lot of practice. She thinks of giving him lessons, but again she reminds herself of the real reason that he is here. *He thinks she is a prostitute!*

She tries not to cum, but she cannot help it. He is moving around her cunt with so much enthusiasm that she cannot hold herself back from creaming in his mouth. She is actually shaking, the thought that this was different but nice, taking her by her pubic hairs and pulling hard. He needs to fuck her now and be done with it, and then he needs to get the fuck out of her apartment so that she can be left to hate herself in peace. He is still eating her cunt out, though, oblivious it seems to the massive amounts of cream escaping it and making its way into his mouth.

He moves her to the couch when it is obvious that she cannot remain standing for much longer. He lays her down carefully, and then places his thick finger into her pussy. She actually likes it. There is a moment where she allows herself to think that he picked her up in the bar without his initial question and that she actually wants to fuck him. Strangely, she does want to fuck him. She wants to feel what it is like to be fucked by someone who is in no way guarded by ego.

When he starts to move his finger around inside her, she is impressed by how into the fucking she is now. He adds another finger and she is close to blowing again, so close in fact that she has to place a hand on his hand to stop him from moving his fingers around inside her. He doesn't stop, though, and soon enough she is cumming again. She cannot believe how good this man with the stocky fingers and fat cock feels.

At last, he mounts her, and she checks to see that he has a condom on. He says that he will pull out in time, and she knows that she has heard this story too many times before. She wriggles out from under him and goes to her side table. She returns quickly with the rubber, and then slides it over his shaft. She gets on her couch again, and again he is on top of her. He fumbles around for a moment and then she feels him inside her. There is a thrill that overcomes her too, and she knows that this has nothing to do with the size of the cock inside her.

He thrusts hard. Short, deep strokes that make her feel like he wants to deposit his cock inside her belly. This is not possible, though, and she knows this, so she just relaxes into this heaviness. And his thrusts are heavy, probably from his weight, and she is quickly enjoying this too. There really is something to be said about a grateful fuck, and this guy is really very grateful.

He thrusts until she cums again, and then he brings himself to blow, he falls on her with all his weight and leaves his dick inside her for the longest time. When it starts to go soft, he extracts it from her and asks where the bathroom is, needing to sort out the condom. Then they gather up their clothing, and he starts to dress. She goes naked to the fridge and comes back with a bottle of champagne, which is all she has in the fridge. She offers him a glass, and he accepts.

They have a subdued chat while drinking the champagne, and then the guy gets up to leave. He doesn't ask her again how much this little tryst will cost him, but after she has let him out, she finds a money clip with ten one hundred dollar bills in it. She laughs to herself and lets it go. She goes to the shower and washes the escapade off her; then she takes the rest of the champagne to bed with her. If she is pregnant, though, she will not be able to be so careless anymore. Tonight was a wild night. However, she tells herself, and there is nothing that she can do about the champagne, or the fat cock, that she already has in her.

She gets up the next morning and decides to put off the pregnancy test for one more day. What she does decide is that it is time for her to go back to New York and see what her old friends have been up to. She reasons that she will need some sort of a support structure if she is, in fact, pregnant, and there is no better support than the only friends she has, which is back in New York City. She starts to pack up her apartment, slowly, knowing that she has the whole month to do it. She also has a few loose ends to tie up in LA, none of which consist of Ray and Karl Von Helsing.

She arrives back in New York City at the end of the third month, and she is obviously pregnant. It is just three months, but she knows this. Anybody who knew her before would know that there was something up. She stays at a decent hotel for a week and then moves into a child-friendly apartment building close enough to Manhattan to try and establish herself as a stylist there. She knows that Ray will have nothing but good things to say about her, and so she is confident about her ability to make her new business work.

Again she considers whether she should call Karl and let him know that he left her with a little more than she bargained for, but she decides against it. There is nothing to be gained by doing this; she tells herself, and so she does not do it. She takes her phone out and deletes Karl's number, and Ray's too. She knows, however that she will have Ray's number on her resume, but what on earth would she tell her as to her reasons for wanting to see or speak to her husband.

AUTHOR'S NOTE

Readers: I want to expand a few of the stories to see where the characters can be explored further. If there are any of the stories that you would like to read more about again, I'd love to hear from you!

Visit my blog at http://www.jaelynnmccranie.com/

Join my newsletter for free exclusive previews
http://jaelynnmccranie.com/newsletter/

Follow me on Twitter at
http://www.twitter.com/jaelynnmccranie

Like my page on Facebook at
https://www.facebook.com/jaelynnmccranieauthor

Discover my books at major ebook retailers everywhere.